Herbert Charles Elmer

A Discussion of the Latin Prohibitive

based upon a complete collection of the instances from the earliest times

to the end of the Augustan period

Herbert Charles Elmer

A Discussion of the Latin Prohibitive
based upon a complete collection of the instances from the earliest times to the end of the Augustan period

ISBN/EAN: 9783337402440

Printed in Europe, USA, Canada, Australia, Japan

Cover: Foto ©Andreas Hilbeck / pixelio.de

More available books at **www.hansebooks.com**

A DISCUSSION

OF

THE LATIN PROHIBITIVE,

BASED UPON A COMPLETE COLLECTION OF THE INSTANCES
FROM THE EARLIEST TIMES TO THE END OF
THE AUGUSTAN PERIOD.

By H. C. ELMER,

Assistant Professor of Latin in Cornell University.

Reprinted from the American Journal of Philology, Vol. XV, 2 and 3.

ITHACA, N. Y.
1894.

TABLE OF CONTENTS.

PART I.

(EXPRESSIONS THE PROHIBITORY CHARACTER OF WHICH IS BEYOND QUESTION.)

PART II.

(EXPRESSIONS ADMITTING OF MORE THAN ONE INTERPRETATION.)

APPENDIX.

THE LATIN PROHIBITIVE.

PART I.

This paper owes its origin to a feeling the writer has long had that certain uses of the Latin perfect subjunctive are very inadequately and, in some particulars, very inaccurately treated in Latin grammars. It is customary, for instance, in dealing with *ne* and the 2d person subjunctive in prohibitions, to dismiss the subject with the statement that when the prohibition is addressed to no definite person, the present tense is used; otherwise the perfect. All attempts—like Gildersleeve's,[1] for instance—to make any further distinction between the tenses have been frowned down. Scholars in general have been inclined to accept the views of Madvig (Opusc. acad. altera, p. 105)[2] and of Weissenborn (on Livy 21, 44, 6) as final, viz. that the perfect is used, when a definite person is addressed, only because the present cannot be used. The reason for this remarkable state of things they do not trouble themselves to seek. Even Schmalz, in the second edition of his Lat. Synt., §31, would have it understood that the perfect tense in this use has no special significance. Such ignoring of all distinction between tenses is common also in other constructions, e. g. in the so-called potential subjunctive.

---

[1] Latin Grammar, §266, Rem. 2, which is, as far as it goes, in perfect harmony with the results reached in this paper.

[2] Madvig is inexcusably careless in some of his statements in this connection. On p. 105, e. g., he says that *ne* with the present is *apud ipsos comicos rarissimum et paene inusitatum*. As a matter of fact, it is extremely common *apud comicos*—far more so than any other form of prohibition.

One of the latest grammars (Allen and Greenough, §311) says that in *aliquis dicat* and *aliquis dixerit* the two tenses *refer without distinction* to the immediate future. The same grammar, in dealing with modest assertion, draws no distinction between *putaverim* and *putem*. It is customary, again, to dismiss the perfect subjunctive in prayers with the mere statement that it is a reminiscence of archaic formulae, without a hint that the perfect necessarily means anything. It has seemed to me that this looseness of interpretation is entirely at variance with the facts of the language, and I have accordingly undertaken an investigation of the whole range of those independent constructions of the perfect subjunctive in which that tense deals with future time. I have included also in my investigation such uses of the future perfect indicative as are frequently said to be 'equivalent to the simple future.' For the purposes of the paper I have collected and classified all the instances of the uses concerned that are to be found in all the remains of the Latin language up to the end of the Augustan period (except the later inscriptions), together with important parts of Silver Latin. I ought perhaps to say that for four volumes of the Teubner text I accepted a collection of instances made by one of my students. He is, however, one in whose care and accuracy I have great confidence, and I feel sure that his collection is substantially complete.

That part of my investigation the results of which I have chosen for the present paper deals chiefly with the 2d person, present and perfect tenses, of the subjunctive in prohibitions. For the purpose of simplifying the discussion I shall, for the present, exclude the few cases (commonly called prohibitions and classed under *ne* with the subjunctive) introduced by *nec, numquam, nihil* (e. g. *nec dixeris, nec putaveris*). There are so serious objections to explaining any one of those introduced by *nec* (*neque*) in the best prose-writers, and some of those introduced by *nihil, numquam*, as instances of the same construction as that found in *ne feceris*, that I shall leave the discussion of such cases for Part II of my paper.

The impression is very generally given that *ne* with the perfect subjunctive is one of the most common methods of expressing prohibition in the best classical prose. As a matter of fact, it is almost entirely unknown to such prose. It will be understood, of course, that the Letters of Cicero do not represent the usage of what is understood by 'classical prose.' Tyrrell has clearly shown that the diction and constructions in the Letters are the diction and constructions of the early comic drama, and not at all those of what is commonly meant by Ciceronian Latin. Indeed, Cicero himself calls especial attention to the wide difference in this respect between them and his other productions in ad fam. IX 21, 1 Quid enim simile habet epistola aut iudicio aut contioni? ... Epistolas vero cottidianis verbis texere solemus. We must not consider these Letters in determining the usage of the best classical prose, any more than we should the usage of early comedy: they, as well as the comedy, reflect the language of familiar every-day life. Throwing the Letters aside, we may say that *ne* with the 2d person perfect subjunctive does not occur in any production, whether prose or poetry, of the whole Ciceronian period, except in seven dialogue passages of Cicero where the tone distinctly sinks to that of ordinary conversation, or unceremonious ordering.[1] If, in addition to these, we except four instances in Horace, we may say that it does not occur between Terence and Livy. It is not to the point to say that a prohibition is in its very nature familiar, nor would such a statement be true. The orations and the philosophical and rhetorical productions of Cicero, as well as the productions of other writers belonging to the same period, abound with prohibitions. The orations of Cicero alone contain 81 prohibitions (or probably twice this number if we count such expressions as *quaeso ne facias, obsecro ne*, etc.), and still in his orations no instance can be found of *ne* with the perfect subjunctive except in pro Murena 31, where Cicero is quoting the supposed words of a teacher to his pupil.

Again, the grammar-rule which says that the present tense is used when the prohibition is general, i. e. addressed to no one in particular, while the perfect is used when it is addressed to some particular person, or persons, is entirely misleading in the form in which it is given. The grain of truth which the rule contains is rendered useless by the absence of any hint as to the principle involved. Sometimes general prohibitions take the perfect tense, e. g. Cato de agri cultura 4 ne siveris; 37, 1 ne indideris; 45, 2 ne feceris; 93 ne addideris; 113, 2 ne siveris; 158, 2 ne addideris; 161, 2 ne sarueris; XII Tabulae, quoted in Serv. in Verg.

---

[1] There is no manuscript authority whatever for *ne siris* (Catullus 66, 91). The manuscript reading *non siris* is the true one. This matter will be fully discussed in Part II of my paper.

Ecl. 8, 99 Unde est in XII tabulis: "Neve alienam segetem pellexeris"; Cic. pro Murena 31, 65 Etenim isti ipsi mihi videntur vestri praeceptores et virtutis magistri, fines officiorum paulo longius, quam natura vellet, protulisse ... "Nihil ignoveris": immo aliquid, non omnia. "Misericordia commotus ne sis": etiam, in dissolvenda severitate: sed tamen est laus aliqua humanitatis (quoting general precepts of the '*vestri praeceptores*' which had just been mentioned. Notice the singular verb side by side with *vestri* (instead of *tui*), which seems to show that the prohibition is general); Hor. Sat. 2, 2, 16 Quae virtus et quanta, boni, sit vivere parvo discite ... hic inpransi mecum disquirite. Cur hoc? Dicam, si potero ... seu pila velox ... seu te discus agit ... sperne cibum vilem; nisi Hymettia mella Falerno *ne biberis* diluta. On the other hand, it is probable that prohibitions addressed to definite persons occasionally take the present tense at all periods of the literature, and that this use is not, even in classical times, confined to poetry, as is commonly supposed. At any rate, there are passages in prose which it requires ingenuity or violence to explain in any other way, and which, if found in Plautus or Terence, no one would have thought of explaining in any other way. This use is very common in early comedy, and I have collected the following instances from Cicero and later prose: Cic. in Verr. II 4, 23, 52 Scuta si quando conquiruntur a privatis in bello ac tumultu, tamen homines inviti dant, etsi ad salutem communem dari sentiunt. *Ne* quem *putetis* sine maximo dolore argentum caelatum domo quod alter eriperet protulisse; ib. de republica 6, 12, 12 "St! quaeso," inquit, "*ne* me e somno *excitetis* et parumper audite cetera" (where the imperative '*audite*' instead of a subordinate subjunctive makes it probable that *ne excitetis* is also independent); id. ad fam. 1, 9, 23 Quod rogas, ut mea tibi scripta mittam, quae post discessum tuom scripserim, sunt orationes quaedam, quas Menocrito dabo, neque ita multae; *ne pertimescas;* ib. 16, 9, 4 Reliquom est, ut te hoc rogem et a te petam: *ne* temere *naviges*—solent nautae festinare quaestus sui causa—cautus sis, mi Tiro—mare magnum et diffi-cile tibi restat—si poteris, cum Mescinio (naviges)—caute is solet navigare (where *cautus sis* and the form taken by the rest of the sentence show that *ne naviges* also is probably independent); id. ad Att. 9, 18, 3 "Tu malum," inquies, "actum *ne agas*" (a proverb applied here to a particular person); id. ad Quintum fratrem 1, 4, 1 Amabo te, mi frater, *ne* ... *adsignes* (Cicero never uses

amare in this sense with a dependent clause, though its paren-
thetical use is common in his Letters with independent imperative
constructions, e. g. ad Att. 2, 2, 1 cura, amabo te, Ciceronem;
ib. 16, 16*c* Amabo te, da mihi et hoc; ib. 10, 10, 3; ad Quint. 2,
8, [10])[1]; Phil. II 5, 10 *ne putetis* (most naturally taken as independent); Livy 44, 22 Vos quae scripsero senatui aut vobis habete
pro certis. Rumores credulitate vestra *ne alatis*, quorum auctor
nemo exstabit (This, or some reading which involves the same
construction, seems inevitably correct, and would undoubtedly
be accepted by everybody were it not for the supposed rule);
ib. 22, 39, 2 Armatus intentusque sis, *neque* occasioni tuae *desis
neque* suam occasionem hosti *des* (Livy and later writers freely
use *neque* for *neve*); Tac. Dialogus 17 Ex quo colligi potest et
Corvinum ab illis et Asinium audiri potuisse (nam Corvinus in
medium usque Augusti principatum, Asinius paene ad extremum
duravit). *Ne dividatis* saeculum, et antiquos ac veteres vocitetis
oratores quos eorundem hominum aures adgnoscere ac velut
coniungere et copulare potuerunt. It was formerly customary
among editors of the Dialogus to punctuate this sentence as
above. Recent editors use only a comma or a semicolon before
ne dividatis, understand an ellipsis (i. e. *Haec dico ne*, etc.), and
thus make Tacitus use a very awkward sentence. Why make
this so difficult? Why not let it be what it seems to be on the
face of it, namely, a prohibition?

Here, then, are several instances in prose of the present subjunctive with *ne* addressed to a definite person. The reason why it
is not more common will appear later on in this discussion. But
even if none of these examples existed (and there have been
ingenious attempts to explain away most of them in deference
to the supposed rule), there would still be no ground for such a
rule. In the whole field of classical prose from the beginning of
the Ciceronian period to the end of the Augustan period, and
even later, there is but a single example of *ne* with the indefinite
2d person present subjunctive in a prohibition. There are a few
examples from poetry, but these have no bearing upon the point
in question, as it is everywhere acknowledged that *ne* with the
present is common in poetry even in addressing a definite person.
The single example just referred to is of course the one cited
under this rule, with suspicious uniformity, by all Latin gram-

---

[1] Even in Plautus and Terence *amabo* in this sense is almost invariably
thrown in parenthetically.

mars, viz. Cic. Cato Maior 10, 33, though even here it might be noticed that Cato is speaking to definite persons, addressing at one time Scipio individually, again Laelius, and still again both together. The truth is that a general prohibition in Latin is nearly always expressed by the use of the 3d person, e. g. *ne quis putet*, etc., or some circumlocution introduced by *cavendum est ne*, or the like. It will, I think, be admitted that the above considerations at least cast serious doubt upon the validity of the grammar-rules regarding the use of *ne* in prohibitions. The question as to the true distinction between the tenses in such constructions seems to me to be still an open one, and this paper is intended as a contribution to its solution.

Let us start with certain general principles. All will agree that the perfect subjunctive, when dealing with a future act, differs, at least in some uses, from the present in representing the act as one finished in the future. For instance, in the expression *si venerit, videat* the act of coming is conceived of as a finished act in the future, about to be completed prior to the beginning of the act of seeing. In *si veniat*, on the other hand, the act is conceived of as in progress in the future. Such a distinction between the tenses of *ne feceris* and *ne facias* would not be entirely satisfactory at all points of the parallel. *Ne feceris* cannot mean literally 'Do not prior to a certain point in the future, have done it.' In one respect, however, the distinction, it seems to me, still holds. In *ne feceris* there is at least no thought of the progress of the act. The expression deals with an act in its entirety. The beginning, the progress and the end of the act are brought together and focussed in a single conception. The idea of the act is not dwelt upon, but merely touched, for an instant, and then dismissed. The speaker, as it were, makes short work of the thought. There is a certain impetus about the tense. When a man says *ne facias* he is taking a comparatively calm, dispassionate view of an act conceived of as one that will possibly *be taking place* in the future; *ne feceris*, on the other hand, implies that the speaker cannot abide the thought; he refers to it only for the purpose of insisting that it be dismissed absolutely as one not to be harbored. As far as the comparative vigor of the two expressions is concerned, the difference in feeling between them is similar to that between 'Go!' and 'Be gone!' 'Go' dwells upon the progress of the act. A man never says 'Be gone!' except when aroused by strong emotion, which does not allow him to think of the progress of the act, but only the prompt accomplishment of it. In a similar way *ne feceris* betrays stronger feeling than *ne facias* —it disposes of the thought with the least possible ado. The same distinction should be made between *cave feceris* and *cave facias*. This feature of the tense, if my characterization of it is correct, would lead us to expect it to be used only, or chiefly, in animated, emotional, or unusually earnest discourse, and to such passages, as we shall presently see, is it almost exclusively confined. I wish to insist upon this as the only real distinction between the two tenses with *ne*. We shall now, of course, expect that in the majority of cases where a prohibition is a general, indefinite one, the present tense will be found. When a man is soberly philosophizing and writing precepts for the world at large, he is not often aroused by emotions so strong as he is when, actually face to face with a person and perhaps under the influence of anger, alarm or some other intense feeling, he orders that person not to do a certain thing. But even in this sort of writing, when he feels that his precept is of prime importance, he may occasionally fall into the more vigorous form of expression. For the satisfactory study of such expressions we look for some production abounding in general precepts, and still not written in the form of dialogue and not addressed to any one in particular. Naturally we turn to Cato's de agri cultura. In the seven different passages of this work cited above, Cato uses *ne* with the perfect in a general prohibition. In each case the context makes it probable, or, in the light of facts which I shall present later, practically certain, that he considers of especial importance the particular thing prohibited, e. g. ch. 4, where he is trying to show how a farmer may live happy and prosperous: ruri si recte habitaveris, libentius venies: fundus melior, minus peccabitur, fructi plus capies. Frons occipitio prior est: vicinis bonus esto: familiam *ne siveris* peccare. Si te libenter vicinitas videbit, facilius tua vendes, operas facilius locabis etc., i. e. '*above all things, do not allow* the members of your household to offend them. If you keep on good terms with your neighbors, you will find it easier to sell your produce,' etc.; again, 37, 1: 'If you are dealing with land that is *cariosa*, peas are a bad crop to put in; so are barley, hay, etc.; *above all things, do not put in nuts (nucleos ne indideris).*' Everywhere else in his treatise he uses the less vigorous forms of prohibition, sometimes *nolito* with the infinitive, sometimes *ne* with the

2d imperative, sometimes *caveto* with the present tense of the subjunctive. He never uses the perfect tense with *caveto*, though this tense with *cave* is far more common in Plautus than the present. The present tense, on the other hand, occurs in Cato 17 times.

By far the best place to study the difference in meaning between the two tenses is in Plautus and Terence, because in them (and only in them) both tenses are very freely used with *ne* and *cave* in prohibitions. It is there, too, that the tone of the prohibition can best be determined, because the dramatic action makes clear the feeling of the speaker. I give below classified lists of all the passages in Plautus and Terence containing prohibitions of this sort.[1] In studying these lists, there are certain considerations which should be kept constantly in mind. In all but a comparatively few cases, the distinction I have drawn between the perfect and the present tenses will be very clear. But of course some instances, both of the perfect and of the present, will be found near the border-line. In some cases where the speaker is moved by only slight emotion, one tense would be as appropriate and natural as the other. Again, a speaker may be somewhat aroused while still under perfect self-control and realizing the advisability of calm language. On the other hand, a speaker may be really very calm, while wishing, for certain purposes, to seem very indignant. We should also bear in mind a natural tendency to unceremoniousness and a vigorous off-hand style in every-day conversation between friends and in the language of superiors to inferiors. If we keep in mind these considerations, a comparison of the following lists will, I think, inevitably lead to the conclusion that the distinction I have drawn is the true one.

There are in Plautus and Terence 31 instances of *ne* with the perfect subjunctive. In nearly all of these the feeling of strong emotion of some sort—e. g. great alarm, fear of disaster if the prohibition is not complied with, or the like—is very prominent. Many of them are accompanied by other expressions which betray the speaker's earnestness, e. g. *per deos atque homines, opsecro, hercle*, etc. And there is not one of them in the least inconsistent with my explanation of the meaning of the tense. Plautus has this construction in the following passages[2]: Am. 924

---

[1] I was surprised to find no instance of this use in the tragedies of Seneca, who, I believe, uses only *ne* with the imperative (or *vide ne* with the subjunctive) in prohibitions.

[2] I have not thought it necessary for my present purpose to make a separate class of such aorists as *dixis, parsis*, etc.

Per dexteram tuam te, Alcumena, oro, opsecro te, da mi hanc veniam, *irata ne sies* (evidently here the perfect of *irascor*. The fact that this verb is inchoative in form does not militate against the principle I have laid down, as it is seldom inchoative [never so, if we may trust Harpers' Dict.] in meaning. It commonly means to *feel angry*. When the beginning of the act is referred to *incipio*, or a verb of similar meaning is used with it, e. g. ad Att. 4, 1, 8 *incipiunt irasci*. Inchoative verbs are not found in this construction); Miles 283 Sc. Nescis tu fortasse, apud nos facinus quod natumst novom. PAL. Quod id est facinus? Sc. Impudicum. PAL. (not wanting to hear such news) Tute sci soli tibi : Mihi *ne dixis*. Notice the many indications of earnest feeling : *Tute* (*tu* alone even would have been emphatic) *soli tibi*, and all sharply contrasted with *mihi*; ib. 862 Perii: excruciabit me erus . . . Fugiam hercle . . . *ne dixeritis*, opsecro, huic vostram fidem! ib. 1333: Here Philocomasium has just fainted and fallen into the arms of her lover, at the thought of leaving him. All is excitement. One says: Run for some water. The lover exclaims: *ne interveneris*, quaeso, dum resipiscit; Rudens 1155 Perii in primo praelio: mane! *ne ostenderis!* Here his possession of the treasure that has been found depends, as he thinks, upon its not being shown; Trin. 521 Per deos atque homines dico, *ne* tu illunc agrum tuom *siris* umquam fieri; ib. 704 (Lysiteles in a quarrel with Lesbonicus, indignant at the suggestion of anything which might reflect upon his character) Id me commissurum ut patiar fieri *ne* animum *induxeris;* ib. 1012 *Ne destiteris* currere (addressed to himself in fear of a flogging. All his words at this point indicate hurry and alarm); Asin. 839 SON (in a tone of earnest deprecation, in answer to his father's taunt): *Ne dixis* istuc. FATHER: *Ne* sic *fueris:* ilico ego non dixero; Curc. 599 PLANESIUM (to Phaedromus, in great fear lest the parasite escape with the stolen ring) . . . propera! . . . Parasitum *ne amiseris!* Pseud. 79 Id quidem hercle *ne parsis!* Most. 1083 THEOPROPIDES (angry, and resolved to punish Tranio, trying to get him away from the altar, where he had taken refuge): Surge . . . *ne occupassis*, opsecro, aram . . . surgedum hinc . . . surge: ne nugare. Aspicedum; Men. 415 *Ne feceris!* periisti, si intrassis intra limen; ib. 617 PE. (during an angry dispute) At tu *ne* clam me *commessis* prandium. ME. Non taces? PE. Non hercle vero taceo; Epid. 150 (in answer to Stratippocles' intimation that he would commit suicide) *ne feceris!* ib. 593 PER. Si hercle te umquam audivero me patrem vocare, vitam tuam ego interimam. FID. Non voco ... *ne fueris* pater; Poen. 552 (the lawyers, speaking with professional decisiveness and importance) Nos tu *ne curassis!* scimus rem omnem. The tone assumed here by the speakers may be inferred from the fact that they have just been accused of speaking with too much anger (cf. vs. 540 nimis iracundi estis); ib. 990 *ne parseris;* Aul. 100 (Euclio having a large amount of gold concealed in his house, is constantly alarmed lest it be stolen. He bids his servant again and again not, under any circumstances, to let any one enter the house) Si bona Fortuna veniat, *ne intromiseris!* ib. 577 EUC. (still in fear of losing his treasure) *Ne* in me *mutassis* nomen! ib. 737 LYC. (upon Euclio's threatening him with death) *Ne* istuc *dixis!* ib. 790 *Ne* me uno digito *adtigeris*, ne te ad terram, scelus, adfligam! Cas. 2, 6, 52 ST. Praecide os tu illi! Age! CLE. (trying to prevent a fight) *Ne obiexis* manum! Cist. 1, 1, 111 Silenium (speaking of her lover, with great depth of feeling that moves her hearers to tears [vs. 113]) sed, amabo, tranquille; *ne* quid, quod illi doleat, *dixeris!* The following seems near the borderline, one tense being as appropriate as the other: Merc. 396 ne duas *neu* te advexisse *dixeris.*

Terence has only two instances of *ne* with the perfect: Phorm. 514 Unam praeterea horam *ne oppertus sies.* The speaker is fairly beside himself throughout this scene, which sufficiently accounts for the more emotional form of expression. Ib. 742 (alarmed by fear lest his treachery be discovered) *Ne* me istoc posthac nomine *appellassis.*

The same feeling that prompts the use of the perfect tense in the passages just cited, explains the use of the same tense in prohibitions introduced by *cave.* Plautus and Terence present 33 instances of *cave* with the perfect: Plaut. Am. 608; Miles 1125; 1245; 1368; 1372; Trin. 513; 555; Asin. 256; 467; 625; Bacch. 402; 910; 1188; Stich. 284; Most. 388; 508; 795; Men. 996; Epid. 400; 434; Merc. 112; 476; Poen. 1020; Aul. 90; 600; 610; Persa 388; 933; Cas. II 5, 24; Ter. And. 753; 760; Haut. 187; Adelph. 458.

If now we turn to *ne* and *cave* with the present subjunctive we find a very different state of things. There are in Plautus and Terence more than 100 instances of *ne*, and 18 (19?) instances of *cave*, in this form of prohibition, as will be seen by consulting the following list: Am. 87 (Prologue addressing the audience) Mirari nolim vos, quapropter Juppiter nunc histriones curet. *Ne mire-mini*[1]: ipse hanc acturust Juppiter comoediam; ib. 116 (still addressing the audience) *Ne* hunc ornatum meum *admiremini;* Capt. 14 Ego me tua causa, *ne erres*, non rupturus sum (probably *ne* here means 'lest'); ib. 58 (Prologue) *Ne vereamini*, quia bellum Aetolis esse dixi cum Aleis; ib. 186: The parasite (replying to Hegio, who has good-humoredly warned him not to expect too much at his table): Numquam istoc vinces me, Hegio: *ne postules* cum calceatis dentibus veniam; ib. 331 Filius meus aput vos servit captus: eum si reddis mihi, praeterea unum nummum *ne duis;* ib. 349 Nec quemquam potes mittere ad eum quoi tuom concredat filium audacius. *Ne vereare:* meo periculo ego huius experiar fidem; ib. 393 Istuc *ne praecipias*, facile memoria memini; ib. 854 Nec nihil hodie nec multo plus tu hic edes, *ne frustra sis;* ib. 947 At ob eam rem mihi libellam pro eo argenti *ne duis:* gratiis a me ducito; ib. 957 Fui ... bonus vir numquam neque frugi bonae neque ero umquam: *ne* spem *ponas* me bonae frugi fore; Miles 1215 Py. Libertatem tibi ego et divitias dabo, si impetras. Pa. Reddam impetratam ... At modice decet. *Ne sis cupidus;* ib. 1274 Viri quoque armati idem istuc faciunt: *ne* tu *mirere* mulierem; ib. 1360 Pa. Muliebres mores discendi. Py. Fac sis frugi. Pa. Iam non possum: amisi omnem lubidinem. Py. I, sequere illos: *ne morere;* ib. 1378 *Ne* me *moneatis:* memini ego officium meum; ib. 1422 Aliter hinc non ibis: *ne sis frustra;* Rud. 941 Nil habeo, adulescens, piscium: *ne* tu mihi esse *postules;* ib. 968 Gr. Hunc homo nemo a me feret: *ne* tu te *speres.* Tr. Non ferat, si dominus veniat? Gr. Dominus huic, *ne* (probably = 'lest') *frustra sis*, nisi ego nemo natust, hunc qui cepi in venatu meo; ib. 992 Quod in mari non natumst neque habet squamas *ne feras;* ib. 1012 Hinc tu nisi malum frunisci nil potes, *ne postules;* ib. 1368 Ut scias gaudere me, mihi triobulum ob eam *ne duis;* ib. 1385 Quod servo meo promisisti, meum esse oportet. *Ne* tu, leno, *postules;* ib. 1390 Dae. Opera mea haec tibi sunt servata: (Gr. Immo hercle mea, *ne* tu tua *dicas*); ib. 1414 nihil hercle hic tibi, *ne* tu *speres;* Trin. 16 (Prologue, to audience) de argumento *ne expectetis* fabulae; ib. 267 Apage sis amor. Amor, amicus mihi *ne fuas* umquam; ib. 370 Ph. ... quid dare illi nunc vis? Lu. Nil quicquam, pater: Tu modo *ne* me *prohibeas* accipere, siquid det mihi; Bacch. 747

[1] Some of these might be explained as final clauses ('that you may not be surprised,' I make the following statement, etc.).

... quod promisisti mihi te quaeso ut memineris, *ne* illum *verberes*
(probably a dependent clause); ib. 758 ... ubi erit adcubitum
semel, *ne* quoquam *exurgatis*, donec a me erit signum datum;
Curc. 183 PA. Quin tu is dormitum? PH. Dormio: *ne occla-*
mites; ib. 213 Si amas, eme: *ne rogites;* ib. 539 *Ne* mihi te
facias ferocem aut supplicare *censeas;* ib. 565 Nil aput me
quidem. *Ne facias* testis: neque equidem dehibeo quicquam;
ib. 568 Vapulare ego te vehementer iubeo: *ne* me *territes;* ib.
713 Non ego te flocci facio: *ne* me *territes* (the feeling in such
cases is not that the failure to comply with '*ne territes*' will be
disastrous to me, but that it will do you no good to try to frighten
me); Ps. 275 ... scimus nos te qualis sis: *ne praedices;* ib. 1234
Sequere tu. Nunc *ne expectetis*, dum domum redeam; Stich.
320 Tua quod nil refert, *ne cures;* ib. 446 ... id *ne* vos *mire-*
mini, homines servolos potare etc.; Most. 598 Pater advenit ...:
is tibi et faenus et sortem dabit. *Ne* inconciliare nos porro
postules; ib. 611 TRA. Huic debet Philolaches paulum. THEOP.
Quantillum? TRA. Quadraginta minas. THEOP. Paulum id
quidemst? TRA. *Ne* sane id multum *censeas;* ib. 799 Ergo
inridere *ne videare* et gestire admodum; ib. 994 Ad cenam *ne*
me te vocare *censeas;* ib. 1010 THEOP. Minas tibi octoginta
argenti debeo. SI. Non mihi quidem hercle: verum si debes,
cedo.... *Ne* ire initias *postules;* Men. 327 *ne* quo *abeas* longius
ab aedibus; ib. 790 Quid ille faciat, *ne* id *observes;* Epid. 147
EP. A quo trapezita peto? STRAT. Unde lubet. Nam ni ...
(prompseris), meam domum *ne inbitas;* ib. 305 *Ne abitas*, priusquam ego ad te venero; ib. 339 [hoc quidem iam periit, *ne* quid
tibi hinc in spem *referas* (perhaps dependent)]; Merc. 164
CHAR. Quid istuc est mali? ACAN. *Ne rogites;* ib. 318 DEM.
Ne me obiurga. LYS. ... non obiurgo. DEM. At *ne* deteriorem
hoc facto *ducas* (there seems to be slight emotion here; either
tense would seem appropriate); ib. 396 *Ne duas* neu te advexisse
dixeris (this, like the passage just cited (vs. 318), seems on the
border-line. The speaker is really very earnest, but is, as shown
by the general situation, anxious not to appear too much so, lest
his real motive be guessed. The sudden change of tense, then,
is not surprising); ib. 457 Ad portum *ne bitas*, dico iam tibi
(perhaps dependent); ib. 520 Nunc, mulier, *ne* tu *frustra sis,*
mea non es; *ne arbitrere;* Poen. 520 *Ne* tuo nos amori servos
esse addictos *censeas;* ib. 526 *Ne* tu *opinere* (perhaps dependent);
ib. 536 Est domi, quod edimus, *ne* nos tam contemptim *conteras*

(perhaps dependent upon 'I say this,' understood); ib. 1152 Audin tu, patrue? Dico, *ne* dictum *neges* (perhaps dependent)'; ib. 1370 *Ne mirere*, mulieres, quod eum sequontur; Aul. 166 Verba *ne facias*, soror; ib. 231 EUCL. At nihil est dotis quod dem. MEG. *Ne duas*, dum modo morata recte veniat, dotatast satis. EUCL. Eo dico, *ne* me thensauros repperisse *censeas*. MEG. Novi; *ne doceas;* ib. 350 Sunt igitur ligna, *ne quaeras* foris; Persa 141 Numquam hercle hodie hic prius edis, *ne frustra sis;* Truc. 477 *Ne exspectetis*, spectatores, meas pugnas dum praedicem; ib. 658 *Ne* me morari *censeas;* ib. 744 Res ita est, *ne frustra sis;* Cas. Prol. 64 (to audience) *Ne exspectetis* etc.; ib. II 6, 42 *Ne* a me *memores* malitiose de hac re factum, aut *suspices;* Cist. II 3, 16 Nam illaec tibi nutrix est: *ne* matrem *censeas;* ib. V (to audience) *Ne expectetis*, spectatores etc. In Capt. 548 Hegio, hic homo rabiosus habitus est in Alide: *ne* tu quod istic fabuletur auris *inmittas* tuas, and in Miles 1363 (1351) PA. Si forte liber fieri occeperim mittam nuntium ad te: *ne* me *deseras*, there seems to be a certain amount of emotion, but it will be noticed that in each case the speaker is addressing a superior. In the former case, too, the speaker is anxious to appear calm and undisturbed. Furthermore, *ne* might well be taken here in the sense of 'lest.' In the other passage, the slave who is speaking does not even mean what he says. He is really glad that he is going, and never wants to see again the master whom he is addressing. In the light of this fact, *ne deseras* seems cool irony. The stereotyped formula *ne molestus sis* occurs in Plaut. Asin. 469; Ps. 118; 889; Most. 74; 572; 757; 863; 871; Men. 251; Aul. 450; but in nearly all of these instances it might be taken as dependent upon some other verb expressed or understood. In any case, one must not look for strong emotion in so commonplace a phrase. *Ne* with the present subjunctive occurs in Terence in the following passages: And. 704 Huic, non tibi, habeo, *ne erres* (perhaps dependent); ib. 706 Dies hic mihi ut satis sit vereor ad agendum: *ne* vacuom esse me nunc ad narrandum *credas;* ib. 980 (to audience) *Ne exspectetis* dum exeant huc; Eun. 76 Quid agas? nisi ut te redimas captum quam queas minimo: ... et *ne* te *adflictes;* ib. 212 Ego quoque una pereo, quod mihi est carius: *ne* istuc tam iniquo *patiare* animo; ib. 273 GN. Quia tristis es. PA. Nihil quidem. GN. *Ne sis;* ib. 388 Si certumst facere, faciam: verum *ne* post *conferas* culpam in me; ib. 786 Sane quod tibi nunc vir videatur esse hic, nebulo magnus est: *ne metuas;* ib. 988 Ere, *ne* me *spectes:* me inpulsore haec non facit; Haut. 745 Sy. Ancillas ... traduce huc propere. Dr. Quam ob rem? Sy. *Ne quaeras;* Phorm. 419 "Actum" aiunt *"ne agas";* Hec. 342 Non visas? *Ne mittas* quidem visendi causa quemquam; Adelph. 22 *Ne exspectetis* argumentum fabulae. In Phorm. 508 Heia, ne parum leno sies, the *ne*-clause is rightly explained by editors as dependent 'Look out there, lest,' etc. Besides these, there are five instances of *ne attigas* which will call for comment later.

Cave with the present tense of the subjunctive occurs as follows: Plaut. Capt. 431; 439; Most. 797; 1012; Epid. 432; Persa 52; 812; Cas. III 1, 16; Poen. 117; Ter. Eun. 751; Haut. 302; 826 (?); Phorm. 993; Adelph. 170.

There are certain remarkable differences between the prohibitions in this latter list (expressed by the present tense) and those in the former list (expressed by the perfect) which a casual observer might not notice. If my distinction between the two tenses is correct, we should expect that a prohibition dealing with mere mental action, e. g. 'Do not suppose,' 'Do not be surprised,' 'Do not be afraid,' would commonly take the present tense, because such prohibitions would not commonly be accompanied by strong emotion, and, as far as the interests of the speaker are concerned, it matters little whether the prohibition be complied with or not. Such a condition of things is exactly what we find. Among the instances of *ne* with the perfect tense, not a single example of a verb of this class will be found; but among those of *ne* with the present there are no less than 31 instances of such verbs, or nearly a third of the entire number. Again, such prohibitions as 'Do not ask me,' 'Do not remind me' (i. e. I know already), would not ordinarily imply any emotion, and no such verbs will be found among the instances of *ne* with the perfect.[1] But there are 13 such verbs among the instances of the present. Substantially the same holds true for the *cave*-constructions. Among the 33 instances of *cave* with the perfect there is no instance of a verb belonging to any of these classes. There is no avoidance of such verbs with *cave* used with the present

---

[1] The nearest approach to an exception is *iratus ne sies* (Plaut. Am. 924), which seems here to be the perfect tense of *irascor*. Here there is an additional idea of venting one's anger, which removes it, strictly speaking, from the class referred to.

tense (in spite of the fact that there are only about half so many instances of the present as of the perfect), e. g. Ter. Phorm. 993; Haut. 826 (*admiratus* here probably used adjectively, as in ad Att. 9, 12, 2 and Off. 2, 10, 35); Plaut. Asin. 372; Capt. 431 (?); or with *noli* (though *noli* is comparatively rare in Plautus and Terence), e. g. Plaut. Persa 619; Capt. 845; Ter. Phorm. 556; or with *ne* followed by the imperative, a construction which occurs 33 times in Plautus and Terence with such verbs (out of a total of 84 instances): Plaut. Am. 674; 1064; 1110; Capt. 554; Miles 893; 895; 1011; 1345; Rud. 688; 1049; Trin. 1181; Asin. 462; 638; 826; Curc. 520; Ps. 103; 734; 922; Men. 140; Merc. 172; 873; 879; 993; Cas. 4, 4, 14; Most. 629; Truc. 496; Aul. 427; Persa 674; Ter. And. 543; Adelph. 279; 942; Haut. 85 (*bis*).[1] Outside of Plautus and Terence such verbs occur, in the ante-Ciceronian period, as follows: Cato de agr. cult. 1, 4 caveto contemnas; ib. 64, 1 nolito credere ('do not believe'); Corpus Inscriptionum Latinarum, I 1445 credere noli; ib. 1453 spernere nolei. But nowhere in this whole period is such a verb to be found in the perfect tense in a prohibition. Why this mysterious absence of all such verbs from this one sort of prohibition? Recurring to the instances of the present tense in Plautus and Terence, we notice that in 11 of the passages the prologue, or some one else, is calmly addressing the audience with 'Do not expect me to disclose the plot of the play,' or some prohibition equally calm. But there is not one instance in the prologues either of Plautus or Terence of the

---

[1] It will be noticed that in Plautus and Terence more than one-third of the verbs in prohibitions expressed by *ne* and the imperative are verbs of fearing (22 of the 33), thinking, asking or advising. Of the remaining verbs, a large proportion are verbs of saying and weeping. A similar state of things prevails in Vergil, who uses this construction 27 times. In 12 of these the verbs belong to the classes just mentioned. All this is interesting in connection with the much-mooted question regarding the relative harshness in Greek of μή with the present imperative and μή with the aorist subjunctive. See Dr. Miller's paper on the Imperative in the Attic Orators, A. J. P. XIII 424. In Latin, *ne* with the perfect subjunctive is harsher than *ne* with the imperative, the latter corresponding rather closely in this respect with *ne* and the present subjunctive. Both of these last-mentioned constructions, however (*ne* with imperat. and *ne* with pres. subj.), smacked somewhat of the same familiar feeling as their sister construction. *Noli* was far more deferential, and Cicero, when he wished to soften the tone of his address, accordingly preferred that form of prohibition.

perfect tense in prohibition. And this again is exactly what we should expect. (It matters little for our present purpose whether Plautus wrote the prologues to his plays or not.) In general the fact may be emphasized that *ne* with the present is chiefly confined to prohibitions of the most commonplace sort. Where this is not apparent from the nature of the verb itself, a study of the context will show that the speaker is not under the influence of any strong emotion. There are in all only 5 instances (a small number out of so many) which can fairly be said to be accompanied by decided emotion, and in each case, strangely enough, the verb is *attigas*, viz. Plaut. Bacch. 445; Most. 453; Epid. 721; Truc. 273; Ter. And. 789. I cannot account for this strange exception, unless one accepts Curtius' suggestion that *attigas* is an aoristic form (Stud. V 433). The few additional passages that might apparently be construed as exceptions have been commented upon under the citation.

Whatever differences of opinion may be held regarding individual instances in the two lists above given, I feel sure that no one who studies them carefully can resist the general conclusion to which I have come. If, now, the distinction I have drawn between the two tenses holds so clearly for the only two authors who make frequent use of *ne* with the subjunctive in prohibitions, a strong presumption is established in favor of a similar distinction in the few instances to be found in later writers, where there are not always so many indications at hand, as in dramatic productions, to make clear the feeling of the writer. And a study of these instances confirms the presumption. There are in classical prose, from the beginning of the Ciceronian period up to near the end of the Augustan period, only seven instances of *ne* with the perfect in prohibition, and these are all in Cicero. As pointed out above, each of these occurs in dialogue where the tone sinks to that of ordinary conversation, in which some one is delivering himself of an earnest, energetic command. One is naturally more unceremonious in addressing a familiar friend than in addressing a mere acquaintance: he falls more readily into energetic forms of expression. Often he assumes an offhand, imperious tone in such cases merely as a bit of pleasantry. This would be especially natural when one was urging his friend not to do what he feared that friend might do—namely, in prohibitions. One can hardly fail to notice this tone at any talkative gathering of intimate friends. Let us examine now more care-

fully the seven instances referred to: de div. 2, 61, 127 (a supposed command of a god to a man) hoc *ne feceris!* de rep. 1, 19,
32 Si me audietis, adulescentes, solem alterum *ne metueritis!* de
leg. 2, 15, 36 (Atticus, replying sharply to Marcus) Tu vero istam
Romae legem rogato: nobis nostras *ne ademeris!* Ac. 2, 40, 125
(in conversation with Lucullus at a familiar gathering of friends)
Tu vero ista *ne asciveris neve fueris* commenticiis rebus adsensus!
Tusc. disp. 1, 47, 112 (replying in a deprecatory tone to a suggestion that has just been made) Tu vero istam *ne reliqueris!*
pro Mur. 31, 65 (quotation from the supposed command of a
teacher to his pupil) misericordia *commotus ne sis!* (though *sis*
alone might be looked upon as the verb here, in which case the
construction would belong to the other class); Par. Sto. 5, 3, 41
(in a vigorous protest) tu posse te dicito, debere *ne dixeris*. An
unusually earnest and energetic tone is to be found in each one
of these. Notice, for instance, the strongly contrasted pronouns
and the other indications of strong feeling. The reason why this
construction is so rare in classical productions is that they are, for
the most part, of a very dignified character. The prohibitions
they contain are therefore commonly expressed by *noli* with the
infinitive (a construction that occurs 123 times in Cicero, twice in
Nepos, three times in Sallust, three times in Caesar), or by *cave*
with the present subjunctive (30 times in Cicero, once in Nepos,
once in Sallust), or by *vide ne* with the subjunctive (18 times in
Cicero, once in Nepos). Next to *noli*, the most common form of
prohibition in Cicero is, I should say, some circumlocution like
peto, rogo, oro, etc., followed by *ne* and the subjunctive, but I
have made no attempt to collect the instances. Even *ne* with
the present subjunctive is less deferential than the constructions
just named; it smacks somewhat of its sister construction, and so
is comparatively rare. Where, next to the early comedy, do we
find the most familiar tone prevailing? One may answer, without
hesitation, in the Letters of Cicero. And it is in these Letters
that most of the instances of *ne* with the perfect in classical times
are found. It is also a significant fact, and one, I think, not
hitherto noticed, that all but 2 of the 14 instances here found
are addressed to his bosom-friends or relatives: 8 of them to
Atticus, 2 to his brother Quintus, and 2 to his intimate legal
friend Trebatius, upon whom he was always sharpening his wits
and whom he never lost an opportunity to abuse, good-naturedly,
to his face. One of the two exceptions is in a very impassioned

passage of a letter written by Brutus to Cicero, ad Brut. 1, 16, 6 ; the other is in ad fam. 7, 25, 2, where Cicero is enjoining upon Fadius Gallus, in the most urgent terms possible, not under any circumstances to reveal a certain secret. To his other correspondents he uses only *noli* or, in two instances, *cave* with the present subjunctive, e. g. to Servius Sulpicius (ad fam. 4, 4, 3), to Lucius Mescinius (ad fam. 5, 21, 1), to Cornificius (ad fam. 12, 30, 1 ; 12, 30, 3), to Gallus (ad fam. 7, 25, 1 ; 7, 25, 2), to Brut. 1, 6 twice; 1, 7 ; 1, 13; 1, 15, 1 twice, etc. Excepting the passionate remonstrance referred to in a letter written by Brutus, the correspondents of Cicero use only *noli* when addressing him, e. g. ad fam. 4, 5, 5 ; 7, 29; 12, 16, 1. In the treatise ad Herennium, I might add, *ne* never occurs in prohibition, though other forms of prohibition are common, e. g. *noli* in 4, 30, 41 ; 4, 41, 53 twice ; 4, 52, 65; 4, 54, 67 ; *cave*, or *vide, ne* with the present subjunctive in 4, 3, 5 ; 4, 4, 6. Following is a complete list of the instances of *ne* with the perfect in Cicero's Letters, nearly all of which show great earnestness, either real or assumed : ad Att. 2, 5, 1 Etiam hercule est in non accipiendo non nulla gloria : qua re si quid Θεοφάνης tecum forte contulerit *ne* omnino *repudiaris ;* ib. 5, 11, 7 nam illam νομανδρια (?) me excusationem *ne acceperis;* ib. 9, 9, 1 Quod vereri videris ne mihi tua consilia displiceant, me vero nihil delectat aliud nisi consilium et litterae tuae ; qua re fac, ut ostendis : *ne destiteris* ad me quicquid tibi in mentem venerit scribere : mihi nihil potest esse gratius (Notice the emphatic position of words, indicative of strong feeling); ib. 10, 13, 1 Epistola tua gratissima fuit meae Tulliae, et mehercule mihi : semper secum aliquam (?) adferunt tuae litterae. Scribes igitur ac, si quid ad spem poteris, *ne demiseris.* Tu Antoni leones pertimescas cave ; ad Brut. 1, 16, 6 Me vero posthac *ne commendaveris* Caesari tuo, ne te quidem ipsum, si me audies. Valde care aestimas tot annos, quot ista aetas recipit, si propter eam causam puero isti supplicaturus es; ad fam. 7, 17, 2 Hunc tu virum nactus, si me aut sapere aliquid aut velle tua causa putas, *ne dimiseris;* ib. 7, 25, 2 Sed heus tu . . . secreto hoc audi, tecum habeto, *ne* Apellae quidem, liberto tuo, *dixeris;* ad Quint. 1, 4, 5 Sin te quoque inimici vexare coeperint, *ne cessaris;* non enim gladiis tecum, sed litibus agetur ; ad Att. 1, 9 *ne dubitaris* mittere ('Do not for a moment hesitate,' etc.); ib. 4, 15, 6 Veni in spectaculum, primum magno et aequabili plausu—sed hoc *ne curaris;* ego ineptus, qui scripserim ; ib. 7, 3, 2 Quin nunc ipsum non dubitabo rem tantam abicere, si id erit rectius; utrumque vero simul agi non potest, et de triumpho ambitiose et de re publica libere. Sed *ne dubitaris* quin, quod honestius, id mihi futurum sit antiquius; ad Quintum fratrem 2, 10, 5 Iocum autem illius de sua egestate *ne sis aspernatus* (Cicero is here speaking of Caesar, which sufficiently accounts for his vigorous tone). In ad Att. 16, 2, 5 Planco et Oppio scripsi equidem, quoniam rogaras, sed, si tibi videbitur, *ne* necesse *habueris* reddere, we should have expected the present. Here, however, it might be noticed that the first hand of the Medicean manuscript (M), the highest possible manuscript authority and in fact the only authority of much importance, omits the *ne*. In ad fam. 7, 18, 3 Tu, si intervallum longius erit mearum litterarum, *ne sis* admiratus, *sis* is probably the verb, *admiratus* being here used adjectively, as in ad Att. 9, 12, 2 sum admiratus ('I am surprised'), and in Off. 2, 10, 35 ne quis sit admiratus etc.

Most of the instances to be found, in the prose of classical times, of *ne* with the 2d person present subjunctive in prohibitions have been cited earlier in this paper. The following should be added to complete the list: Cic. Cato Maior 10, 33 *ne requiras;* ib. ad Att. 2, 24, 1 *ne sis* (*perturbatus* perhaps here used adjectively, like the following *sollicitus* and *anxius*). There are a large number of other passages that might well be explained as instances of the same use, e. g. ad Att. 14, 1, 2 Tu, quaeso, quicquid novi scribere *ne pigrere* (which Madvig, Opus. 2, p. 107, and Kühner, Lat. Gram. II, §47, 8, actually explain as independent of *quaeso*); Phil. II 5, 10; pro Cluentio 2, 6 *ne repugnetis* etc. That *ne* with the present subjunctive is not more common in the best prose is due to an increasing fondness for the *noli*-construction. *Ne* with the present was a mild prohibition as compared with *ne* with the perfect, but it was less deferential and respectful than *noli*, and in dignified address *noli* accordingly became the regular usage. In early comedy there was comparatively little call for the more calm and dignified forms of expression, and there accordingly we find that *noli* is comparatively rare. It occurs in Plautus and Terence only in addressing some one who must be gently handled. It is found only where the tone is one of pleading—it never conveys an order, in the strict sense of that word. It is almost never used by a superior in addressing an inferior. In the two or three exceptions to this rule, the superior has some motive for adopting the mild tone. Those who wish to test the truth of these remarks are referred to the following complete list of the instances of *noli* in Plautus and Terence: Plaut. Am. 520; 540; Capt. 845; Miles 372; 1129; Trin. 627; Asin. 417; Curc. 128; 197; 697; Most. 800; Merc. 922; Poen. 367; 871; 1319; Persa 619; 831; Truc. 664; Cas. II 2, 32; II 6, 35; Cist. I 1, 59; I 1, 109; Ter. And. 385; 685; Phorm. 556; Hec. 109; 316; 467; 654; Adelph. 781.

As regards the different forms of prohibition in classical times, nothing can show more strikingly the difference in feeling between *ne* with the perfect subjunctive and *noli* with the infinitive than a comparison of the classes of verbs found in the two constructions. Of the 123 instances of *noli* in Cicero, 76 of them are used with verbs indicating some mental action, or some action which would be as unlikely to be accompanied by emotion on the part of the speaker, e. g. 'Do not suppose,' 'Do not be afraid,' etc.[1] In the Letters, 21 out of the 32 instances are verbs of this sort. Of the 30 instances of *cave* with the subjunctive, 17 are of this sort.[2] In the Letters the proportion is 11 out of 18. A glance at the instances above cited of *ne* with the present subjunctive will show that most of the verbs in this construction also belong to the same class. We found the same state of things also in Plautus and Terence. Now, side by side with these facts put the fact that in the whole history of the Latin language, from the earliest times down to and including Livy, there are to be found in prohibitions expressed by *ne* with the perfect subjunctive only two, or at most three, verbs denoting mere mental activity, viz. *ne dubitaris* (Cic. ad Att. 7, 3, 2), *ne metueritis* (de rep. I, 19, 32), *ne*

[1] Planc. 18, 44; 19, 46; 19, 47; 20, 50; 21, 51; 22, 52; 22, 53; Balb. 28, 64; Pis. 20, 46; 27, 66; Marcel. 8, 25; Ligar. 11, 33; 12, 37; Phil. 2, 28, 69; 7, 8, 25; 12, 6, 14; de or. 2, 47, 194; 2, 61, 250; 2, 66, 268; Brut. 33, 125, 40, 148; nat. deor. 2, 18, 47; Cato 22, 79; Rosc. Am. 24, 67; in Caec. div. 12, 39; Verr. 2, 1, 16, 42; 2, 1, 49, 128 (twice); 2, 2, 11, 29; 2, 2, 51, 125; 2, 3, 5, 11; 2, 3, 46, 109; 2, 4, 5, 10; 2, 4, 51, 113 (twice); 2, 5, 5, 10; 2, 5, 18, 45; 2, 5, 53, 139; de re pub. 1, 41, 65; 2, 3, 7; Orat. prid. quam in exsil. iret 1, 1; Tusc. disp. 5, 5, 14; imp. Pomp. 23, 68; agr. 2, 6, 16; 2, 28, 77; Mur. 19, 38; 37, 80; Flacc. 20, 48; 42, 105; Sull. 16, 47 (twice); 27, 76; de dom. 57, 146; de harusp. responso 28, 62; ad Att. 1, 4, 3; 2, 1, 5; 5, 2, 3; 6, 1, 3; 6, 1, 8; 8, 12, 13; 9, 7, 5; 12, 9; 13, 29, 2; 15, 6, 2; 16, 15; ad Brut. 1, 13, 2; ad fam. 4, 4, 3; 4, 5, 5; 5, 21, 1; 7, 25, 1; 12, 16, 1; 12, 33; ad Quint. 1, 2, 4, 14; 3, 6, 7 (twice).

[2] Ligar. 5, 14; 5, 16 (twice); de rep. 1, 42, 65; de leg. 2, 3, 7; Tusc. disp. 5, 7, 19; ad Att. 5, 21, 5; 7, 20, 1; 8, 15, A 2; 9, 9, 4; 9, 19, 1; 10, 13, 1; ad Brut. 1, 15, 1 (twice); ad fam. 7, 6; 7, 25, 2; 9, 24, 4.

curaris (ad Att. 4, 15, 6).[1] The only other verbs (four or five in number) dealing with mental action distinctly involve also other sorts of action. These are *ne sis aspernatus* (ad Quint. fratrem 2, 10, 5), *ne asciveris neve fueris* adsensus (Ac. 2, 40, 125), *commotus ne sis* (pro Mur. 31, 65), and *ne repudiaris* (ad Att. 2, 5, 1). There are not so many objections to regarding *nec existimaveris* in Livy 21, 43, 11 as a prohibition as there would be in Ciceronian Latin, though it is extremely doubtful even here. In any case, nothing of the sort should cause surprise in Livy, as he marks the beginning of a general breaking up of the strict canons observed in the best period. Livy (3, 2, 9) even goes so far as to say *ne timete*, which, in prose, would have shocked the nerves of Cicero beyond expression. The almost entire avoidance, until after the Augustan period, of this whole class of verbs expressing mere mental activity in prohibitions expressed by *ne* with the perfect subjunctive, and its remarkable frequency in other forms of prohibitions, can, it seems to me, be explained only in one way. Verbs of this class are, from their very nature, such as would not often be accompanied with passionate feeling, and so are confined to the milder forms of expression. And this, it seems to me, goes far to establish my contention that *ne* with the perfect subjunctive is reserved for prohibitions that are prompted by uncontrollable emotion, or else that are intended to be as vigorous as possible in tone, either, as is generally the case, from some serious motive, or merely as a bit of familiar pleasantry. This tone is commonly one of commanding. Rarely it is one of earnest entreaty, though in such cases the prohibition is commonly introduced by *noli*. *Noli* with the infinitive is the expression best calculated to win the good-will of the hearer, as it merely appeals to him to exercise his own will (i. e. 'Be unwilling'), or to forbear using it; while *ne* with the perfect subjunctive disregards altogether the will of the person addressed, and insists that the will of the speaker be obeyed.

---

[1] *Ne necesse habueris reddere* (ad Att. 16, 2, 5) is but poorly supported by manuscript evidence. Even if the reading is correct, as seems highly probable, the idea of *reddere* may be said to figure quite as prominently in the prohibition as that of *habueris*. Such expressions as *ne vos quidem timueritis* (Cic. Tusc. Disp. 1, 41, 98), *numquam putaveris* (Sall. Iug. 110, 4) and *nec putaveris* (Cic. Acad. 2, 46, 141) represent very different uses, as I shall show in Part II of my paper.

In Part I of this paper I confined myself exclusively to prohibitions introduced by *ne, cave* and *noli.* That the clauses there discussed were *bona fide* cases of prohibition admitted of no doubt, with the exception of a few introduced by *ne* which might possibly be explained as dependent. Unfortunately, grammars are wont to classify under the same head, and with equal confidence, certain other forms of expression, many of which can be shown to belong to very different uses of the subjunctive mood. Most prominent among these are the instances of

Neque (nec) with the Perfect (Aorist) Subjunctive.

Before proceeding to discuss these clauses, let us get them all before us. As my statistics for this particular construction have, as far as the Augustan poets are concerned, been rather hurriedly gathered, I do not feel sure that my list contains all of the instances from those writers; but the few omissions, if there are any, could not affect the results reached. My statistics show that the following are the only instances of the construction to be found, from the earliest times down to the end of the Augustan period, which any one would ever think of explaining as prohibitions: Plaut. Capt. 149 Ego alienus? alienus ille? Ah, Hegio, numquam istuc dixis *neque animum induxis* tuom; Trin. 627 Sta ilico. Noli avorsari *neque* te *occultassis* mihi[1];

Enn. Ann. 143 (Baehrens) nec mi aurum posco *nec* mi pretium *dederitis;*

Lucil. Sat. 30 (Baehrens 775) —∪∪—∪∪— "*neque* barbam *inmiseris* istam!"

Ter. And. 392 Hic reddes omnia, quae nunc sunt certa ei consilia, incerta ut sient, sine omni periclo: nam hoc haud dubiumst,

---

[1] The *videris* in Plaut. Mil. 573 (Ne tu hercle, si te di ament, linguam comprimes posthac: etiam illut quod scies nesciveris *nec videris* quod videris) is probably in the future perfect indicative (cf. the preceding *comprimes*). This use of the future perfect is very common in Plautus and Terence.

quin Chremes tibi non det gnatam. *Nec* tu ea causa *minueris* haec quae facis, ne is mutet suam sententiam; id. Haut. 976 Nemo accusat, Syre, te : *nec* tu aram tibi *nec* precatorem *pararis;* Cic. Acad. 2, 46, 141 Nihil igitur me putatis moveri? Tam moveor quam tu, Luculle, *nec* me minus hominem quam te *putaveris;* id. Fin. 1, 7, 25 Quid tibi, Torquate,... quid tanta tot versuum memoria voluptatis adfert? *Nec* mihi illud *dixeris:* "Haec enim ipsa mihi sunt voluptati et erant illa Torquatis"; id. pro Sulla 8, 25 Aut igitur doceat Picentis solos non esse peregrinos aut gaudeat suo generi me meum non anteponere. Qua re *neque* tu me peregrinum posthac *dixeris*, ne gravius refutere, neque regem, ne derideare; id. Brutus 87, 298 nam de Crassi oratione sic existimo, ipsum fortasse melius potuisse scribere, alium, ut arbitror, neminem; *nec* in hoc ironiam *dixeris* esse, quod eam orationem mihi magistram fuisse dixerim; id. Rep. 6, 23, 25 Igitur alte spectare si voles atque hanc sedem et aeternam domum contueri, *neque* te sermonibus volgi *dederis nec* in praemiis humanis spem *posueris* rerum tuarum; id. ad Att. 12, 23, 3 Si nihil conficietur de Transtiberinis, habet in Ostiensi Cotta celeberrimo loco, sed pusillum loci, ad hanc rem tamen plus etiam quam satis: id velim cogites. *Nec* tamen ista pretia hortorum *pertimueris.* Nec mihi iam argento nec veste opus est nec quibusdam amoenis locis; id. ib. 13, 22, 5 Alteris iam litteris nihil ad me de Attica; sed id quidem in optima spe pono: illud accuso, non te, sed illam, ne salutem quidem. At tu et illi et Piliae plurimam, *nec* me tamen irasci *indicaris;* id. ad Att. 15, 27, 3 Quod me de Bacchide, de statuarum coronis certiorem fecisti, valde gratum, *nec* quicquam posthac non modo tantum, sed ne tantulum quidem *praeterieris;* id. ad fam. 1, 9, 19 ... recordare enim, quibus laudationem ex ultimis terris miseris. *Nec* hoc *pertimueris;* nam a me ipso laudantur et laudabuntur idem; id. ad Att. 10, 18, 2 Tu tamen perge quaeso scribere *nec* meas litteras *exspectaris,* nisi cum quo opto pervenerimus, aut si quid ex cursu ;

Hor. Od. 1, 11, 3 Tu ne quaesieris quem mihi, quem tibi finem di dederint, Leuconoe, *nec* Babylonios *temptaris* numeros; id. Sat. 1, 4, 41 Primum ego me illorum dederim quibus esse poetas excerpam numero: *neque* enim concludere versum *dixeris* esse satis; neque si qui scribat, uti nos, sermoni propiora, putes hunc esse poetam (cf. *dederim,* vs. 39);

Verg. Ecl. 8, 102 Fer cineres, Amarylli, foras rivoque fluenti transque caput iace, *nec respexeris;*

Ovid, Am. 2, 2, 25 ... ne te mora longa fatiget, inposita gremio
stertere fronte potes. *Nec* tu ... *quaesieris;* id. H. 8, 23 ...
nupta foret Paridi mater, ut ante fuit. *Nec* tu *pararis* etc.; id.
Epist. 19, 151 Si nescis, dominum res habet ista suum. *Nec* mihi
credideris; id. Ar. Am. 1, 733 Arguat et macies animum. *Nec*
... *putaris* etc.; id. ib. 2, 391 Gloria peccati nulla petenda sui est.
Nec dederis etc.; id. ib. 3, 685 Sed te ... moderate iniuria turbet,
nec sis audita pelice mentis inops. *Nec* cito *credideris* etc.; id.
Met 12, 455 Memini et venabula condi inguine Nesseis manibus
coniecta Cymeli. *Nec* tu *credideris* etc.; id. Trist. 5, 14, 43 Non
ex difficili fama petenda tibi est. *Nec* te *credideris* etc.; id. ex
Pont. 1, 8, 29 Ut careo vobis, Scythicas detrusus in oras, quattuor
autumnos Pleïas orta facit. *Nec* tu *credideris* etc.; id. ib. 4, 10,
21 Hos ego, qui patriae faciant oblivia, sucos parte meae vitae, si
modo dentur, emam! *Nec* tu *contuleris* urbem Laestrygonis
etc.; id. Fasti 6, 807 Par animo quoque forma suo respondet in
illa, et genus et facies ingeniumque simul. *Nec* quod laudamus
formam tu turpe *putaris;*

Tibull. 2, 2, 13 Iam reor hoc ipsos edidicisse deos. *Nec* tibi
malueris etc.; id. 4, 1, 7 Est nobis voluisse satis, *nec* munera
parva *respueris;*

Propert. 3, 13 (20), 33 (Müller) ... tumque ego Sisyphio saxa
labore geram. *Nec* tu supplicibus me *sis venerata* tabellis; id.
3, 28, 33 ... cur reus unus agor? *Nec* tu virginibus reverentia
moveris ora ;

Livy 5, 53, 3 ego contra—*nec* id *mirati sitis*, priusquam quale
sit audieritis—etiam si tum migrandum fuisset incolumi tota urbe,
nunc has ruinas relinquendas non censerem; id. 21, 43, 11 ...
"hic dignam mercedem emeritis stipendiis dabit." *Nec* quam
magni nominis bellum est, tam difficilem *existimaritis* victoriam
fore; id. 23, 3, 3 Clausos omnis in curiam accipite, solos, inermis.
Nec quicquam raptim aut forte temere *egeritis;* 29, 18, 9 Quibus,
per vos fidem vestram, patres conscripti, priusquam eorum scelus
expietis, *neque* in Italia *neque* in Africa quicquam rei *gesseritis*,
ne ... luant.

I have included the instances of this use from Early Latin in
the above list, for the sake of completeness and for the purpose of
facilitating comparison with what I have to say regarding the
construction in classical times; for the following remarks will be
chiefly concerned with classical prose. It will be observed that
there are twelve instances of this use in Cicero—five of them

outside of his Letters. It seems to have been taken for granted that these are examples of the same construction as that in the prohibitive *ne feceris*. Grammars cite them side by side with the last-mentioned construction, often without so much as a comment. See, e. g., Madvig, 459, obs.; Roby, 1602; Gildersleeve, 266, rem. 1; Draeger, Hist. Synt., §149 B *b* (p. 313); Allen and Greenough, 266 *b*; Riemann, Syntaxe latine (Paris, 1890), p. 483; Schmalz-Landgraf in Reisig's Lat. Vorlesungen, p. 482; Schmalz, Lat. Synt., §31; Kühner, Ausführl. Gram. d. lat. Sprache, II, §§47, 9; 48, 3; 48, 4; etc., etc. And still they bear upon their face a suspicious look. What is *nec* doing in such a very pronounced and direct expression of the will in Cicero? Apart from these particular expressions, all grammarians agree that *neque* (*nec*), in the sense of *neve* (*neu*), is extremely rare in classical prose. I shall presently try to show that it does not occur at all in any volitive expression outside of poetry until the beginning of the period of decline, with the possible exception of one instance in Nepos. And still the grammars, even the most recent of them, would give us to understand that Cicero (of all writers!), in adding a prohibition in the perfect subjunctive, invariably, except in one passage, uses *neque* (*nec*). *Neve* (*neu*) with the perfect subjunctive occurs only once in Cicero in a prohibition. And we are asked to believe that *neque* (*nec*) occurs twelve times! Let us see whether such a state of things really exists.

Evidently our best starting-point in attempting to discover to what extent *neque* (*nec*) was used in prohibitions will be found in expressions whose prohibitive character is beyond all question, viz. expressions in which the verb is in the imperative, or, if in the subjunctive, is preceded by another verb which itself is introduced by *ne* or *neve*. The use of *ne* or *neve* will show beyond all possibility of doubt that the mood of the verb is volitive in character. Without the presence of such a *ne* or *neve*, one may often claim the right at least to doubt any one's interpretation of the mood of a given verb as volitive in meaning. For instance, when Cicero says (Ac. 2, 46, 141) ... tam moveor quam tu, Luculle, *nec* me minus hominem quam te *putaveris*, there is nothing to show that *nec* ... *putaveris* does not mean 'nor would you for a moment suppose that I am less human than you.' But, if we had such a sentence as *ne* ... *dixeris, nec putaveris*, we could hardly escape the conclusion that *nec putaveris* must be in the same construction as *ne dixeris*.

What is to be said, then, of the use of *neque* (*nec*) with the imperative prior to the period of Cicero, in whom the passages under discussion are found? Merely this, that it does not once occur in any production, whether prose or poetry, of the whole ante-Ciceronian period. In the same period *neve* (*neu*) with the imperative occurs 121 times. These instances are nearly all in the laws, i. e. in prose: Corpus Inscriptionum Lat. I 28 (three times); 197 (eight times); 198 (twelve times); 199 (three times); 200 (thirty-four times); 204 (five times); 205 (three times); 206 (forty-five times); 207 (once); 576 (twice); 1409 (twice). Other instances are XII Tabulae, X 1 ne ... *neve urito;* Plaut. Stich. 20 ne lacruma *neu face;* Cato, de agri cult. 144, 1 *neve facito.* Sometimes the *ne* is repeated: Ter. Heaut. 84 and 85 ne retice, *ne verere.* An examination of the Ciceronian period discloses the same condition of things, except that there does seem to be one clear instance of this use of *nec* in Catullus 8, 10.[1] It still remains very rare during the first half of the Augustan period. Horace has it once, Od. 2, 7, 19. Possibly there are two other instances in Horace, viz. Od. 1, 9, 15 Quem fors dierum cumque dabit, lucro adpone *nec dulces amores sperne*, puer, *neque* tu *choreas*, though here it might be said that the negatives connect merely the substantives, and the negative idea for the verb is allowed to take care of itself; and Od. 3, 7, 29 Prima nocte domum claude *neque* in vias sub cantu querulae despice. In this last passage it may be that it is not so much the idea of *despice* that is negatived as that of *in vias.* There is no objection to the act of looking down, but it must not be *in vias.* This use is also very rare in Vergil, though *neve* with the imperative is very common in his writings. By the time, however, of Tibullus, Propertius and Ovid, the old distinction between *neque* (*nec*) and

[1] The following instances must not be confused with this use: Cic. ad Att. 12, 22, 3 Habe tuom negotium, *nec* quid res mea familiaris postulet sed quid velim *existima;* id. Leg. 3, 4, 11 Qui agent auspicia servanto, auguri publico parento, promulgata, proposita, in aerario cognita agunto, *nec plus quam* de singulis rebus *semel consulunto*, rem populum docento etc. . . . Censores fidem legum custodiunto; privati ad eos acta referunto *nec eo magis* lege liberi *sunto.* In the first of these passages the idea of the verb is not negatived at all. The meaning is 'Think, not this, but that.' In the second passage, similarly, the negative spends its force upon *plus quam* etc., and the meaning is 'they are to consult not more than once.' In the third case, likewise, the meaning is 'and not on this account (whatever other grounds there may be) are they to be free,' etc. Only the first of these passages gives us the words of Cicero, the others being quotations made by him from laws.

neve (neu) had broken down, and the one was used about as freely as the other with the imperative. But from first to last the use remained a poetical license.[1]

The above facts in themselves are enough to prejudice us very decidedly against explaining any *neque (nec)* in Cicero as introducing a prohibition. But let us now turn to *neque (nec)* used in prohibitions expressed by the subjunctive. As before pointed out, we can be sure that the subjunctive in such cases is hortatory in character only when *ne* or *neve (neu)* has preceded. How often, then, does *neque (nec)* occur in such clearly prohibitive uses of the subjunctive mood? Not once in prose from the earliest times till after the Augustan period, and only once in direct address in poetry,[2] Horace being again the poet who first ventures to make the innovation (Od. 1, 11, 2).[3] When a writer wishes to add a second prohibition to one already introduced by *ne*, or *neve*, he does so sometimes by *neu:* Plaut. Merc. 396 ne duas *neu dixeris;* id. Poen. 18 ff. ne sedeat, *neu mutliant, neu obambulet, neu ducat;* id. ib. 30 Ne sitiant *neve obvagiant;* id. 38 ne detur *neve extrudantur;* Cato, de agri cult. 5, 4; ib. 38; ib. 83; ib. 143; Cic. Ac. 2, 40, 125 ne asciveris *neve fueris* adsensus; etc.; sometimes by *aut:* Plaut. Curc. 539 Ne facias *aut censeas;* Ter. Eun. 14 Ne frustretur *aut cogitet;* sometimes by the repetition of *ne:* Ter. Haut. 85 ne retice, *ne verere;* Cato, de agri cult. 5, 2.

Now, with all this evidence before him, one should hesitate long before explaining any *neque (nec)* in Cicero as used with a volitive subjunctive. All other possible interpretations should be tested first. Now let us turn to the passages from Cicero which have prompted these remarks. There are twelve instances in Cicero of *neque (nec)* with the perfect subjunctive, which have been

---

[1] In Livy 22, 10, 5 Si id moritur, quod fieri oportebit, profanum esto, *neque scelus esto*, the meaning may be 'and it shall be no *scelus*.'

[2] Capt. 437 Ne tu me ignores tuque te pro libero esse ducas, pignus deseras, *neque des operam* pro me ut huius reducem facias filium must not be mistaken as illustrating this use. If *neque* here introduced a prohibition, the meaning would be 'and do not give,' which would be the direct opposite of the meaning intended. The *ne* at the beginning forms the prohibition with *des*, as with *ignores, ducas* and *deseras*, and the negative of *neque* merely reverses the meaning of the word *des*. The meaning is 'and do not *not* give,' i. e. 'and do not fail to give,' = *et ne non des.*

[3] With the third person it seems to occur at rare intervals as a poetic license, e. g. Catullus 61, 126.

looked upon as prohibitions. In not one of them has anything preceded that even suggested a prohibition. Most of them are preceded by simple assertions, or questions, in the indicative mood. In those cases where a subjunctive has preceded, the *nec* begins an entirely new sentence, so loosely connected with the preceding that editors separate the two sentences with a period. A striking proof that this use of the perfect subjunctive with *nec* is a construction entirely distinct from that of *ne* with the same mood and tense is found in the fact that certain writers who never use the latter at all are wont to make frequent use of the former. *Ne* with the perfect subjunctive is, for instance, entirely foreign to Ovid, but that poet, as will be seen by consulting the citations given above, uses *nec* with the same mood and tense, in sentences exactly similar in every way to those in Cicero, at least eleven times. The same condition of things exists in Vergil, Tibullus and Propertius, none of these authors making any use whatever of *ne* with the perfect subjunctive, whereas they present repeated instances of *nec* with that mood and tense. Again, this construction is found in the Orations of Cicero, where *ne* with the perfect is never used except once in a quotation, pro Sulla 8, 25; cf. also Verr. 2, 1, 54, 141. But there is other evidence perhaps even more striking than this. It will be remembered that we found, prior to the beginning of the period of decline, only two or three instances of verbs denoting merely mental activity used in prohibitions expressed by *ne* and the perfect subjunctive; while in all other sorts of prohibition such verbs were found in large numbers. We found conclusive proof that this form of prohibition was felt to be unsuited to expressing such mild prohibitions as 'do not think,' 'do not believe,' etc. Refer now to the list above given of *nec* with the perfect subjunctive. Out of the 38 instances there given of this use—a decidedly smaller number than exist of *ne* with the perfect in the same period—15 are of just the sort of verbs that are so uniformly absent from prohibitions expressed by *ne* with that tense. Surely all this looks as though we are on altogether different ground. We shall find later on that the fact that so many verbs denoting mental activity are found with this use of *nec* forms as strong an argument in favor of assigning the use to a certain other class of constructions as it forms against classifying it in the usual way.

There now remains, so far as I can see, only one possible argument which those can use who still prefer the common interpretation of these clauses. It is claimed by our Latin grammars that *neque* (*nec*) is occasionally used in Cicero in other sorts of volitive clauses where it is equivalent to *neve* (*neu*). No less an authority than Schmalz (Revision of Krebs' Antibarbarus, II, p. 121; Revision of Reisig's Vorlesungen, p. 482) expresses this view in very distinct terms. Now, some one may say, if Cicero uses *neque* (*nec*) at all in expressions of the will, as in purpose clauses, there is no reason why he should not use it in any volitive expression. Even if the premises were true, this would hardly seem a fair conclusion to draw from them, but I venture to dispute the premises and to claim that *neque* (*nec*) is never used by Cicero to negative the subjunctive in purpose clauses, or in any other volitive clauses. The proof of this is given by Schmalz's own statistics, and it is surprising that he did not see it.

Before taking up the passages that have been supposed to contain examples of *neque* (*nec*) in volitive clauses, it will be well to remind ourselves of certain facts which must be kept constantly in mind. The most important of these facts is this : that every purpose clause is, at the same time, a result clause as well. When a man says : 'I wish to train my children properly, that they may, in after years, be honored citizens,' their being honored citizens is, to be sure, the purpose of his training, but it may also be conceived of merely as the future result of that training. The use of the word 'that' instead of 'so that,' and 'may' instead of 'will,' shows that in this particular instance the purpose idea is probably uppermost in the mind of the speaker. Suppose now he says : 'I wish to train my children properly, *so that* (i. e. to train them in such a way that) they *will*, in after years, be honored citizens.' The two sentences practically mean the same thing, and one might at any time be substituted for the other; but in the second the substitution of 'so that' and 'will' shows that the feeling uppermost in the mind is that of result. In cases of this sort the mind may be fixed upon what will be the result of the action, and the idea of purpose that is implied may be left to take care of itself. Now, the Latin language is not fortunate enough, except in negative clauses, to have separate mechanisms in such cases to make clear the predominant feeling. The Latin would express the two ideas 'in order that they may' and 'so that (with the result that) they will' in exactly the same way. It accordingly very frequently happens that it is impossible to determine whether a clause introduced by *ut* is to be classed as a purpose clause or a result clause. Such, for instance, are the following sentences: ... omni contentione pugnatum est, *uti* lis haec capitis *aestimaretur* (Cic. Cluent. 41, 116); Conscios interfecit *ut* suom scelus *celaretur* ('that his crime might be concealed' or 'so that his crime was concealed'); ... exarsit dolor. Urgere illi, *ut* loco nos *moverent;* factus est a nostris impetus; etc. It is true that what precedes an *ut*-clause commonly shows whether the coming *ut*-clause is to be felt as a purpose clause or a result clause; but it is also true that it very frequently does not. More than that: it often happens (and this is of especial importance in this connection) that what precedes would lead one to expect that a result clause is to follow, when a final clause, or some other kind of volitive clause, actually does follow. Such a sentence is found, for instance, in Ter. Phorm. 975 Hisce ego illam dictis *ita tibi incensam* dabo, *ut ne restinguas,* lacrimis si extillaveris. The expression *ita tibi incensam dabo* ('I will render her so enraged at you') might lead one to expect the thought to be completed by a clause of result, viz. ut *non* restinguas etc. = 'that you will not appease her anger, if you cry your eyes out.' Instead of that, the thought is shifted, and the sentence is completed, as the *ne* clearly shows, by an expression of the will. The meaning of the passage then is: 'I will make her so enraged at you, that you *shall* not ('shall,' instead of 'will,' denoting determination rather than mere futurity) appease her anger,' etc.[1]

Such expressions of determination, purpose and the like, where a result clause might commonly be expected, are not at all infrequent. Such a shifting of feeling cannot, of course, be detected when the subordinate clause is affirmative; but where that clause is negatived, the choice between the negatives *ne* and *non* will show, beyond all question, the predominant feeling of the clause. I have made no attempt to collect passages illustrating this particular point, but Brix has made a collection of such passages

---

[1] I should not deem it necessary to stop to interpret the *ne* in this and similar passages, had not so distinguished a scholar as Brix, in my opinion, wholly misunderstood it. Misled by preconceived notions as to what ought to follow such expressions as *ita tibi incensam dabo*, he makes the statement (ad Plaut. Mil. 149) that *ne* and *ut ne* are sometimes used "nicht nur in Final-, sondern auch in Consecutivsätzen."

from Plautus and Terence in his note on Plaut. Mil. Gl. 149.[1] In
any one of these passages, all of which are cited and discussed in
my note appended below, *ut non*, instead of *ne* or *ut ne*, would be
perfectly possible and would, in fact, have been expected, but the
use of *ne*, or *ut ne*, shows that the contents of the *ut*-clause were
looked upon not primarily as a result of anything, but rather as

[1] Brix cites the passages as illustrations of the consecutive use of *ne* and *ut
ne*, but it will be noticed that in each case the *ne*, or the *ut ne*, may, without
violence, and in fact without the least difficulty, be interpreted as involving
in some form a distinct expression of the will; and, if this is the case, surely
there can be no possible excuse for explaining it differently. Here are the
passages, in the order in which Brix gives them: Mil. Gl. 149 ... eum ita
faciemus *ut*, quod viderit, *ne viderit*, 'will manage him so that he *shall not* have
seen, i. e. shall not think that he has seen,' etc. ('shall not,' instead of 'will
not,' implying that the act is willed by the subject of *faciemus*); id. Capt. 738
Atque hunc me velle dicite ita curarier, *ne* qui deterius huic *sit* quam quoi
pessumest; id. Most. 377 Satin' habes, si ego advenientem ita patrem faciam
tuom, non modo *ne* intro *eat*, verum etiam ut fugiat longe ab aedibus? id.
Bacch. 224 Adveniat quando volt atque ita *ne sit* morae; id. Capt. 267 ne id
quidem involucri inicere voluit, vestem *ut ne inquinet;* id. Men. 1100 Prome-
ruisti *ut ne quid ores*, quod velis quin impetres; id. Trin. 105 Est atque non
est mihi in manu, Megaronides: quin dicant, non est: merito *ut ne dicant*, id
est; id. Mil. Gl. 726 Ita me di deaeque ament, aequom fuit deos paravisse,
uno exemplo *ne* omnes vitam *viverent;* Ter. Hec. 839 Ad pol me fecisse
arbitror, *ne* id merito mihi *eveniret*. It is true that in the instances, cited by
Brix, of *potin ut ne*, the introduction of a volitive feeling is somewhat surprising, but such a turn of the thought is perfectly intelligible and offers not the
slightest excuse for supposing that *ne* is here used in the sense of *non*. (That
such a use did once exist admits of no doubt [cf. *ne ... quidem, ne-scio* etc.], but
reminiscences of this use are not found in cases like those under discussion.)
In Men. 606 Potin *ut* mihi molestus *ne sis*, there is a fusing together of two
expressions; Potesne? mihi molestus ne sis! The feeling that prompts the
speaker's words here may be expressed by 'Cease your annoyance, can't you?'
We might put these same words into the form of a question pure and simple:
'Can't you cease your annoyance?' and if they were uttered with the proper
emphasis and tone, the hearer would understand them at once as a command,
and not at all as a question asking for information. In cases like the above,
then, the choice of *ne* instead of *non* is determined by the feeling of the
speaker, without regard to the grammatical form in which the sentence is cast.
A similar phenomenon is found in the use of *quin*. This word really means
'why not?' and should, strictly speaking, take the indicative, as in Ter.
Heaut. 832 Quin accipis? But 'why don't you take it?' under certain circumstances is felt as really meaning 'take it!', and in such cases *quin* is frequently
found with the imperative, as in Ter. And. 45 Quin tu dic, regardless of the
fact that *quin* is, or was, an interrogative. Similar phenomena are found also
in Greek, where we find μή or μηδέ used even with the future indicative in

an expression of somebody's will. The idea of result is in most cases present, but the mind is fixed primarily upon the idea of will that accompanies it. Clauses similar to those cited from Plautus and Terence are not uncommon in the best classical prose and poetry, as will be seen by consulting Draeger's Hist. Synt. II, §410.

Now, if volitive clauses are so common where result clauses might be expected, we should not be greatly surprised if result clauses are occasionally found where purpose clauses might be expected, especially since the ideas of purpose and result are, confessedly, so closely associated. And it is the failure to recognize this fact that has led grammarians to assert that *neque* (*nec*) is occasionally used in final clauses. As intimated above, the latest champions of the view that this use is found in Cicero are Schmalz and Landgraf, who express it in their revision of Reisig's Vorlesungen, p. 482. But they greatly damage their own side of the question by certain concessions which they make. They even lay stress upon the fact that *neque* (*nec*) is never used in a clause introduced by *ne*, *neve* (*neu*) being the invariable word in such cases. Again, in Schmalz's revision of Krebs' Antibarbarus he says: "An dieser Regel, dass *nec* nie bei Cicero zur Fortsetzung von *ne* dient, muss unbedingt festgehalten.' This is true, despite the bare assertion of Draeger in his Hist. Synt., §543, 7. Schmalz might have made his statement even more sweeping and said that such a use of *neque* (*nec*) does not occur anywhere in the best classical prose. With the exception of one passage in Nepos (Pausanias 4, 6), it remains a strictly poetical license, and extremely rare besides, until the time of Livy. Now, side by side with this fact, let us put certain other facts to which reference has

---

questions which imply a prohibition, e. g. Soph. Tr. 1183 Οὐ θᾶσσον οἴσεις μηδ' ἀπιστήσεις ἐμοὶ 'will you not extend your hand and not distrust me?' This question implies a prohibition, 'extend your hand and *do not distrust me*,' and the fact that the speaker felt it as such accounts for his using μηδέ instead of οὐδέ, which the future indicative would otherwise call for (cf. Goodwin, Moods and Tenses, §299). Such a shifting of the thought inside of a sentence would of course be more common in colloquial language than in dignified styles. It is seen again in Persa 286 Potin ut molestus *ne sis?* In Pseud. 636 Potest ut alii ita arbitrentur et ego *ut ne credam* tibi, the feeling must be 'It is possible that others think so (that you are honest) and that I nevertheless *am not to trust* you,' implying that, from some source or other, he has received the warning *ne credas* 'Do not trust him.' This warning would, from his own point of view, become *ne credam* 'I am not to trust you,' in which, of course, the volitive feeling would still remain.

been made. We found that the clauses now under discussion are really known to be primarily volitive in character only when they are introduced, or accompanied, by *ne* or *neve*. But clauses thus introduced, or accompanied, by *ne* or *neve*, in spite of the fact that they occur everywhere very frequently, present not a single instance, in the best prose, of a second verb added by *neque* (*nec*), such verbs being invariably added by *neve* (*neu*). Is not the inference clear? The few *ut*-clauses continued by *neque* (*nec*) that have been supposed to be purpose clauses are to be interpreted as laying stress rather upon the result idea. Let us apply the interpretation I have suggested to the clauses in question, bearing constantly in mind the serious objection I have pointed out to the common interpretation:

Cic. ad fam. 9, 2, 3 Ac mihi quidem iam pridem venit in mentem bellum esse aliquo exire, ut ea quae agebantur hic quaeque dicebantur, *nec viderem nec audirem*, i. e. 'to escape to some place where I should no longer see, or hear,' etc. ('the result of which flight would be that I,' etc.);

in Caecil. 16, 52 qui si te recte monere volet, suadebit tibi ut hinc discedas *neque* mihi verbum ullum respondeas, i. e. 'will advise you in such a way as to result in your departing without saying a word in reply';

Verr. II 2, 17, 41 Illi eum commonefaciunt ut utatur instituto suo *nec cogat* ante horam decimam de absente secundum praesentem iudicare; impetrant, i. e. 'they earnestly plead with him, *with the result that* he follows his usual custom *and does not compel*, etc.; they thus win their point';

de off. 2, 21, 73 In primis autem videndum erit ei, qui rem publicam administrabit, ut suom quisque teneat *neque* de bonis privatorum publice *deminutio fiat*, i. e. 'he will have to *see to it and bring about the result that*,' etc.;

de off. 1, 29, 102 Efficiendum autem est ut adpetitus rationi oboediant eamque *neque praecurrant nec* propter pigritiam aut ignaviam *deserant*, where *efficiendum* calls particular attention to the result;

Lael. 12, 40 Nulla est igitur excusatio peccati, si amici causa peccaveris; nam, cum conciliatrix amicitiae virtutis opinio fuerit, difficile est amicitiam manere, si a virtute defeceris. . . . aeque autem nefas sit tale aliquid et facere rogatum et rogare. . . . Haec igitur lex in amicitia sanciatur, ut *neque rogemus* res turpis *nec faciamus* rogati. This *ut*-clause has been wrongly explained as volitive in character, because *haec lex* has been supposed to look forward to the *ut*-clause, and *rogemus* and *faciamus* have been looked upon as representing the hortatory subjunctive of the *lex*. But the whole burden of thought in the preceding chapter has been that one should never do wrong even for a friend. *Haec lex* looks backward to the principle there laid down, and the meaning is 'Let this, of which we have spoken, be an established principle in friendship, so that we shall not (i. e. with the result that we shall not) ask a friend to do wrong, nor do it ourselves when asked.'

The three following passages may be considered together: in Verr. II 3, 48, 115 Nunc, ut hoc tempore ea ... praetermittam *neque* eos *appellem*, a quibus omne frumentum eripuit, ... quid lucri fiat cognoscite; id. ib. II 4, 20, 45 Ut *non* conferam vitam *neque* existimationem tuam cum illius, hoc ipsum conferam, quo tu te superiorem fingis; id. de imp. Cn. Pomp. 15, 44 Itaque ut plura *non* dicam *neque* aliorum exemplis *confirmem* quantum auctoritas valeat in bello, ab eodem Cn. Pompeio omnium rerum egregiarum exempla sumantur. These passages involve the same idiom that we have in our 'so to speak.' It is customary to explain the idiom as one developed from the idea of purpose. It may well have started with some such idea, but it drifted so far away from its starting-point that oftentimes there is certainly no idea of purpose left. 'So to speak' becomes merely an apologetic phrase, meaning 'if I may say so,' 'so speaking.' In the first of the passages just cited the meaning is merely 'Now, passing by those, etc., for the present and without calling up those from whom, etc., learn,' etc. As far as the real logical relation of such clauses to the sentences in which they stand is concerned, it is often impossible to conceive of them as purpose clauses at all. When they are meant as such they take *ne* as their negative. But in the clauses above there is no such meaning. In the first clause *neque* was used for the same reason that would have made it appropriate if the expression were *praetermittens neque appellans* (if I may be allowed to use the participle in this way, to illustrate my point); and the choice of negative in the other clauses may be similarly explained. The difference between such clauses as these, and those introduced by *ne* with which they have been classed, will become evident to any one who will examine such a collection of instances as is found in Roby, Lat. Gram. 1660: Cic. ad fam. 15, 19 ne longior sim, vale,

'*in order that I may not become tedious*, I will say good-bye'; id.
Deiot. 1 Crudelem Castorem, *ne dicam* sceleratum et impium, i. e.
'I call him *crudelem, in order to avoid* a harsher term'; etc., etc.
It will be found that the clauses in question cannot be treated in
this manner.

The use of *neque* (*nec*) to connect two verbs in the volitive
subjunctive must be very carefully distinguished from that in
which the negative merely negatives the idea of a single word, or
phrase, in which case the negative is used without reference to
the mood of the verb.   Such clauses are the following:

Cic. de orat. 1, 5, 19 . . . hortemurque potius liberos nostros
ceterosque, quorum gloria nobis et dignitas cara est, ut animo rei
magnitudinem complectantur *neque eis* se aut praeceptis aut
magistris aut exercitationibus, quibus utuntur omnes, *sed aliis
quibusdam*, quod expetunt, consequi posse confidant.   Here the
negative in *neque* does not negative the verb at all, but merely
contrasts the *eis* with the following *sed aliis*, the verb itself being,
like *complectantur*, used in a positive sense ;

Cic. Fin. 4, 4, 9 Quid, quod pluribus locis quasi denuntiant, ut
neque sensuum fidem sine ratione *nec* rationis sine sensibus exqui-
ramus, where the negatives spend their force entirely upon the
phrases *sensuum fidem sine ratione* and *rationis sine sensibus*,
without any regard to the mood of the verb ;

Caes. B. G. 7, 75 ne tanta multitudine confusa *nec* moderari *nec*
discernere suos *nec* frumentandi rationem habere possent, where
the negatives connect the infinitives, without any regard to the
subjunctive.[1]

No objection to this interpretation can be found in the fact that
neve (*neu*) is frequently used in volitive clauses even to negative
single words and phrases, e. g. Cic. de legibus 2, 27, 67 . . . eam
ne quis nobis minuat *neve vivos neve mortuos;* id. ad fam. 1, 9, 19
. . . peto a te, ut id a me *neve in hoc neve in aliis requiras*.
There is, in the first place, a wide difference between such clauses
as these last and the others.   In these last the acts (*eam* . . .

---

[1] The negatives in the following clauses from Early Latin may be similarly
explained, though they seem to be extreme cases: C. I. L. I 196, 10 Magister ⸜
neque vir neque mulier quisquam eset; Plaut. Asin. 854 *Neque divini neque mi
humani* posthac quicquam adcreduas, Artemona, si huius rei me mendacem
esse inveneris; and perhaps Capt. 605 (though this may be explained differently, as will appear later) *Neque* pol me insanum, Hegio, *esse* creduis *neque
fuisse* umquam *neque esse morbum*, quem istic autumat, i. e. 'depend upon it, I
am not crazy, nor have I ever had the disease,' etc.

minuat and *id . . . requiras*) are absolutely negatived—they are not to occur under any conceivable circumstances. In the other passages the act in each case is to take place, but with certain exceptions and restrictions, and it is these exceptions and restrictions that are introduced by the negative in *neque (nec)*. In each case the negative has to do only with its own particular word, or phrase, and is not affected by the character of the clause as a whole. When, however, the feeling of negative volition extends over the whole clause and everything in it, and all the negatives partake of the volitive coloring, we have *neve (neu)*.

There now remain, as supposed instances of *neque (nec)* in volitive clauses, only the following passages, all of which have, in my opinion, been misinterpreted: Cic. de re pub. 1, 2, 3 Et quoniam maxime rapimur ad opes augendas generis humani studemusque nostris consiliis et laboribus tutiorem et opulentiorem vitam hominum reddere . . . teneamus eum cursum, qui semper fuit optimi cuiusque, *neque* ea signa *audiamus*, quae receptui canunt, ut eos etiam revocent, qui iam processerint; Sall. Jug. 85, 47 Quam ob rem vos, quibus militaris aetas est, adnitimini mecum et capessite rem publicam: *neque* quemquam ex calamitate aliorum aut imperatorum superbia metus *ceperit;* Cic. de off. 1, 26, 92 Quae primum bene parta sit nullo neque turpi quaestu neque odioso, deinde augeatur ratione, diligentia, parsimonia, tum quam plurimis, modo dignis, se utilem praebeat, *nec* lubidini potius luxuriaeque quam liberalitati et beneficentiae pareat, though perhaps here the negative in *nec* should be looked upon as negativing merely the idea of *lubidini* and *luxuriae*, as opposed to *liberalitati* and *beneficentiae*. The misinterpretation, as I conceive it, of these passages has been due primarily to the failure to recognize the extent to which a certain class of subjunctives is used in Latin, and this failure, in turn, may be due, in part at least, to a wrong theory regarding the origin of this particular usage. I refer to that use of the subjunctive which deals with expressions of obligation and propriety. Such a use of the subjunctive is hardly recognized at all by grammarians, except in certain questions like, e. g., *cur ego non laeter?* and in certain subordinate clauses like, e. g., *Nihil est cur tibi vera non dicat*. In such clauses the meaning of obligation, or propriety, must of course be recognized by all; and such clauses have been regarded as traceable to a volitive origin. Such questions as *cur ego non laeter?* are looked upon as intimately connected with the deliberative subjunctive, and are put into the same category as *quid agam?* ('what shall I do?'). Any one may see the results of such a treatment by examining Kühner's Ausführl. Grammatik der lateinischen Sprache, Bd. II, §47, 2 *b* (p. 137). Here are gathered together numerous questions in the present subjunctive, all professing to illustrate the deliberative question as a subdivision of the volitive subjunctive; but the surprising thing to my mind is that questions with *ne* and questions with *non* are given side by side as illustrations of the same construction, apparently without the least consciousness that there is any difference in meaning between the two. I wish to protest against the practice of associating together such questions as *quid agam, iudices?* (Cic. Verr. 5, 1, 2), *Ne doleam?* (Cic. ad Att. 12, 40, 2), on the one hand, and *cur ego non laeter?* (Cic. Catil. 4, 1, 2) and *hunc ego non diligam?* *Non admirer?* (Cic. Arch. 8, 18), on the other. It seems to me that all the evidence points to their belonging to entirely distinct uses of the subjunctive mood. The questions of the first class deal with the will. When a man says *quid agam?* ('what shall I do?') he is asking himself or some one else for directions. The answer will be an expression of the will: 'Do so and so.' Similarly, the question *ne doleam?* anticipates from some source or other a prohibition 'I am not to grieve? (are those your commands?).' But the questions of the other set are very far removed from any such meaning. *Cur ego non laeter?* means 'why should I not be glad?' and the answer, so far as any is expected, will be 'you should not (ought not to) be glad for the following reasons,' etc., or 'you should (ought to) be glad,' or the like. Similarly, *hunc ego non diligam?* means 'should I not (ought I not to) love this man?'[1] The will in this last case is not involved in the slightest degree. There is, accordingly, no idea of deliberation in the question. Cicero's mind had been made up long before, and *hunc ego non diligam?* is merely a rhetorical way of saying "surely I ought to love such a man as this." I can find no instance in Latin literature of *non* introducing a question which is truly deliberative in character. Where that negative is used in questions which grammarians have been pleased to call delib-

---

[1] The only explanation of *non* that will prove satisfactory for all the instances concerned is one that regards it as parallel in every way with the *non* in *cur non laeter?* This interpretation may seem more acceptable later on in this paper.

erative, the context shows that the question either is settled already, and so is purely rhetorical in character and equivalent to a negative assertion of obligation, or propriety, or possibility; or else asks for information, anticipating in reply an assertion of obligation, or propriety, or possibility. It never asks for advice, or direction—it never anticipates in reply an expression of the will in any form. In other words, it is never deliberative. We should therefore never expect to find *ne* as a negative in such questions, nor in the answers to such questions, and we never do find it. And here I wish to call attention to a strange error of which Kühner has been guilty. In §47, 2 (pp. 136–7) of his Latin grammar, in speaking of questions of deliberation, he says: "Die Negation ist *ne*." He then proceeds to give a list containing ten negative questions, all of which he calls deliberative and eight of which are *negatived by non*. The two which are negatived by *ne* (both found in the same passage, Att. 12, 40, 2) are not independent questions at all; they depend upon the verb of demanding that has preceded. The truth is that the negative type of the deliberative question, corresponding to the Greek deliberative subjunctive with μή, is not found in the Latin language. The Latin confines its deliberative questions to positives; the Greek frequently gives them a negative form; we in English sometimes combine the two forms, e. g. 'Shall I go, or shall I not?'

While it is true that *non* never occurs in deliberative questions, as a negative of the subjunctive, it is equally true that *ne* never occurs in expressions of obligation, or propriety. The following passages may be referred to as illustrations of negative questions of obligation, or propriety: Plaut. Most. 2, 2, 24; id. Trin. 133; Ter. Hec. 342; And. 103; id. 384; Cic. Vat. 2, 4; Arch. 8, 19; Catil. 4, 1, 2; ad fam. 10, 23, 15; Planc. 7, 18. Many others will be found by consulting Merguet's Lexikon zu Cicero. But, some one will say, these questions are at least developments from the deliberative question, and so go back ultimately to a volitive origin. Of this there is not the slightest evidence. The only thing that can be said, so far as I can see, in favor of such a theory is that one can conceive how such a transition might have taken place.[1]

---

[1] It is barely possible that some one might cite the following passages in support of such a view, inasmuch as they are commonly translated by the use of 'should,' while having *ne* as a negative: Cic. ad Att. 2, 1, 3 ... isdem ex libris perspicies et quae gesserim et quae dixerim: aut *ne poposcisses;* ego

It seems to me that we must regard this use of the subjunctive as connected with the subjunctive used to express the 'would' idea (commonly designated in the grammars as the 'potential'). The two expressions 'no one would think' and 'no one should think' do not lie so far apart that one conception could not readily pass into the other. In fact, it frequently happens that one hesitates whether to use 'would' or 'should' in translating a subjunctive. Such a case is found in Tac. Ann. 3, 50 Studia illi, ut plena vaecordiae, ita inania et fluxa sunt; *nec* quicquam grave ac serium ex eo *metuas*, qui suorum ipse flagitiorum proditor non virorum animis sed muliercularum adrepit. In translating this passage there is really no choice between 'nor would you apprehend anything' and 'nor should you,' etc. That the two ideas are practically equivalent for certain purposes is shown by the fact they are sometimes expressed by the same word in our own language; and it is shown by similar phenomena in at least one other language besides Latin. Our word 'should' may, under certain circumstances, express obligation or propriety, or may represent the conclusion of a condition corresponding to a less vivid future condition in Latin. The sentence 'I should attack the enemy, if my commander should give the order,' may mean 'I ought to attack them' under those circumstances, or it may mean merely that the act *would* occur under those circumstances. Such a transition of thought may also be paralleled from the

---

enim tibi me non offerebam; id. Verr. 2, 3, 84, 195 . . . sin, ut plerique faciunt, in quo erat aliqui quaestus, sed is honestus atque concessus, frumentum, quoniam vilius erat, *ne emisses*, sumpsisses id nummorum, quod tibi senatus cellae nomine concesserat. But these passages do not support any such theory. In the first place, one must look upon *ne poposcisses* and *ne emisses* with suspicion. No other instance of such a use can, I believe, be found— at least before the period of Silver Latinity; and the manuscript evidence in at least one of these passages is somewhat shaky. At any rate, no argument as to the origin of a construction can be based upon one or two curiosities of comparatively late times. If these two instances are to stand, they must be looked upon as purely volitive in character. *Ne poposcisses* and *ne emisses* are simply *ne poposceris* and *ne emeris* from a past point of view—they are prohibitions conceived of in the past. Any one who would insist upon 'you should not have bought' as an accurate translation of *ne emisses* would, to be consistent, have to admit 'you should not (ought not to) buy' as an accurate translation of *ne emeris*. When *ne emisses* is translated by 'you should not have bought,' 'should not' must be understood as merely the past of 'you shall not,' which, despite the original meaning of 'shall,' contains no idea of obligation, but is merely the expression of the speaker's will.

Greek in the use of the so-called potential optative. While such expressions as οὐκ ἄν ... ἀγορεύοις start with the idea 'you would not talk,' this has in Hom. Il. 2, 250, and elsewhere, come to mean 'you should not talk.' See Goodwin's Moods and Tenses, §237. Another proof that the two ideas are readily exchangeable is found in the fact that the place of a Greek potential optative with ἄν, in the conclusion of a condition, is sometimes taken by χρή with the inf. and equivalent expressions (Goodwin's Moods and Tenses, §§502, 555). This is a clear recognition of the practical equivalence in such cases of the potential idea ('would think') and the idea of obligation and propriety. It seems at least as natural, then, to associate together these two uses of the subjunctive as it does to associate the use under discussion with a volitive idea. But I do not care to press further this theory. Let the reader still cling, if he will, to the theory of a volitive origin. In one point we must still agree, and that is that the negative in clauses of obligation and propriety is, from the earliest times to the latest, invariably *non*, and not once *ne*.

This subjunctive of obligation or propriety is the use I referred to above as not having received the recognition it deserves. What good reason is there for limiting such a use of the subjunctive to certain forms of questions and subordinate clauses, when it would suit many other clauses far better than the common interpretation? Is it not, when one stops to think of it, a little strange that grammarians and editors, without a moment's hesitation, translate such questions as *cur non audiamus?* as meaning 'why should we not hear?' and then apparently regard it as impossible that *non audiamus*, without the *cur*, can mean 'we should not hear'? In the question with *cur* the negative is, without exception, from the earliest times *non*—never *ne*—and still, when exactly the same thing is found in a declarative form, grammarians (e. g. Kühner, II, p. 145) and commentators proceed to work out some ingenious theory to show how *non* came to be used where *ne* would have been expected.

If those who are interested in this question will only get rid of the idea that the subjunctive in clauses of obligation or propriety must in some way be associated with the volitive subjunctive, and will then recognize this use as having somewhat freer scope than they have been accustomed to suppose, they will find that many difficulties will be at once disposed of. They will, in the first place, be relieved of the necessity of explaining why those few clauses which they are willing to call clauses of obligation have *non* instead of *ne*. But this will be only a beginning of the satisfaction that their new belief will bring them. The passages from Cicero and Sallust which prompted these remarks will then be perfectly clear and their negatives perfectly regular. The one from the de re pub.: teneamus eum cursum, qui semper fuit optimi cuiusque; *neque* ea signa *audiamus* quae etc., will then mean 'we should keep to that course which has always been that of all good men, and should not heed the signals which,' etc.[1] The *neque quemquam metus ceperit* in Sallust will mean 'nor should any one fear.' Many other difficulties will cease to be difficulties. In Cic. pro Cluent. 57, 155 Quoniam omnia commoda nostra, iura, libertatem, salutem denique legibus obtinemus, a legibus *non recedamus*, the *non recedamus* will mean 'we should not recede.' The negatives in the following passages may be similarly explained: Cic. de re pub. 4, 6, 6 *Nec* vero mulieribus praefectus *praeponatur* . . ., sed sit censor, qui viros doceat moderari uxoribus; id. ad Att. 14, 13 A Patere, obsecro, te pro re publica videri gessisse simultatem cum patre eius: *non contemperis* hanc familiam; honestius enim et libentius deponimus inimicitias rei publicae nomine susceptas quam contumaciae.

The choice of *non* instead of *ne* will now be clearly understood in such passages as the following: Ter. And. 787 Hic est ille: *non* te *credas* Davom ludere; Plaut. Trin. 133 *Non* ego illi argentum *redderem?* Cic. Arch. 8, 18 Hunc ego *non diligam? Non admirer? Non* omni ratione defendendum *putem?* id. 19 Nos . . . *non* poetarum voce *moveamur?* ad fam. 14, 4, 5 Quid nunc rogem te, ut venias, mulierem aegram et corpore et animo confectam? *Non rogem?* Sine te igitur sim? We noticed earlier in this paper that *neque* (*nec*) is not found in Early Latin in clauses that are stamped as volitive in character by the use of an

---

[1] The whole context is distinctly in favor of taking *audiamus* in this sense. There is no instance of any such hortatory expression previous to this in the production, nor on the pages following. On the other hand, there are, in the ten lines next preceding, repeated expressions of obligation denoting what 'we ought to do,' e. g. Ergo ille civis . . . ipsis *est praeferendus* doctoribus; quae est enim istorum oratio tam equisita quae *sit anteponenda* bene constitutae civitati publico iure et moribus? Equidem quem ad modum urbis magnas viculis et castellis *praeferendas* puto, sic eos, qui his urbibus consilio atque auctoritate praesunt, iis, qui omnis negoti publici expertes sunt, longe duco sapientia ipsa *esse anteponendos*.

imperative or by the use of an accompanying *ne* or *neve*. In the face of such a condition of things, one must feel great hesitation in supposing *neque* (*nec*) to be used in any volitive clause during that period. And still, what is to be done with the following? Plaut. Bacch. 476 Ipsus neque amat, *nec* tu *credas;* id. Capt. 149 Ah, Hegio, numquam istuc dixis *neque* animum *induxis* tuom; id. Trin. 627 Noli avorsari *neque* te *occultassis* mihi (This is the only passage in which a clear prohibition of any sort precedes. It does not count for much against the mass of evidence bearing in the other direction, and it is not necessary here to regard *neque occultassis* as a prohibition); Enn. Ann. 143 (Baehrens) Nec mi aurum posco *nec* mi pretium *dederitis;* id. 509 *Nemo* me dacrumis *decoret nec* funera fleta *faxit;* Lucil. Sat. 30 (Baehrens 775) *neque* barbam *inmiseris;* Ter. And. 392 *Nec* tu ea causa *minueris* haec quae facis. The explanation I have suggested clears up all of these passages. The failure to recognize the use of the subjunctive for which I am pleading has repeatedly resulted in the corruption of manuscripts by scholars who could not understand the negative they found there. No less distinguished scholars than Riese and Schmalz are among those to whom I allude. In his admirable edition of Catullus, Riese (followed by Schmalz, Lat. Synt., §31) changes *non siris* to *ne siris* in Catul. 66, 91 Tu vero, regina, tuens cum sidera divam Placabis festis luminibus Venerem, Unguinis expertem *non siris* esse tuam me, sed potius largis adfice muneribus. I am convinced that there is not the slightest evidence of any kind for this reading. The manuscripts, without exception, read *non*. *Ne* with the perfect subjunctive is a construction unknown to Catullus. More than that, it is a construction not found in any poet, except 4 times in Horace, from the time of Terence till after the Augustan Age (and it is rare even then), while the construction involved in my interpretation of the passage is found in every prominent poet of the Golden Age. I showed, too, in Part I of this paper, that *ne* with the perfect is not used in dignified address until Silver Latin. This is true even in Horace, the only poet who uses the construction at all. But the passage in Catullus is addressed to a queen (*regina Berenice*, daughter of Ptolemy Philadelphus), and such a harsh and abrupt address would not be in harmony with the mock-heroic style of the poem.[1] Similar

---

[1] My interpretation is in perfect harmony with the remark of Quintilian in I, 5, 50, of which so much has been made by those who read *ne siris*. See my Appendix.

corruptions have taken place for similar reasons in Rutil. Lup.
II 9 *non credideris;* Sen. Nat. Qu. 1, 3 *non dubitaveris;* Nepos,
Ages. 4, 1 quare veniret *non dubitaret.* On the reading in these
passages cf. Reisig-Haase, Lat. Synt., neu bearbeitet von Schmalz
und Landgraf, p. 481. Manuscripts only too often need to be
delivered from their friends.

We are now ready to return to the passages in Cicero that have
prompted all of these remarks. My explanation of *nec* with the
perfect subjunctive in those passages has, I presume, already been
surmised. They seem to me instances of that particular phase of
the so-called (unfortunately[1]) potential subjunctive which is commonly translated by the use of the auxiliary 'would,' or, in the
first person, 'should.' In applying this test to the various
instances, one must keep in mind that this idea sometimes
approaches that of obligation or propriety, and that in such cases
one need not hesitate, in translating, to use the auxiliary 'should'
instead of 'would.' The subjunctive in Acad. 2, 46, 141 Tam
moveor quam tu, Luculle, *nec* me minus hominem quam te
putaveris, is then to be translated 'nor would you (should
you) for a moment think that I,' etc. Such a translation makes
equally good sense in all the other passages in question. It is
open, so far as I can see, to no objection of any kind. On the
other hand, it receives a striking confirmation at the hands of
Cicero himself. I refer to Cic. Tusc. Disp. 1, 41, 98 *Ne* vos
quidem, iudices, mortem *timueritis.* Grammars (e. g. Roby,
1602; Draeger, Hist. Synt., §149 B; Kühner, Ausf. Lat. Gram.
II, §47, 9, p. 143) are wont to classify this as a prohibition,
instead of taking *ne* and *quidem* together in the sense of 'not
even.' This would be in conflict with two principles I laid down
in Part I of my paper: (1) that the perfect subjunctive is not
used in prohibitions addressed to *iudices*, or in other dignified
prohibitions, and (2) that it is not, except in two or three
passages, used with verbs denoting mere mental activity, before
the period of decline. On these grounds alone I should reject
the interpretation referred to above. But, fortunately, I am not
in the present instance obliged to trust to such deductions. The
whole passage in Cicero is a close translation of chapters 32

---

[1] The term 'potential' ought, it seems to me, to be limited to expressions of
ability and possibility—to the 'can' and the 'may' ideas. I see nothing in
the term 'potential' that makes it appropriate for designating any other
construction.

and 33 of Plato's Apologia Socratis. The part of which the particular sentence concerned is a translation runs as follows: Ἀλλὰ καὶ ὑμᾶς χρή, ὦ ἄνδρες δικασταί, εὐέλπιδας εἶναι πρὸς τὸν θάνατον. The perfect subjunctive is, then, here equivalent to χρή with the infinitive. This, taken in connection with the use, above referred to, of χρή and the infinitive for the potential optative in conclusions of conditions, seems to me to prove beyond all possible doubt that *non timueritis* may, without the least hesitation, be translated by 'you should not fear,' *nec putaveris* by 'nor should you think,' etc., etc., wherever 'should' seems to make a better translation than 'would.'

I have called attention above to the fact that the predominance, in the construction of *nec* with the perfect subjunctive, of verbs denoting mere mental activity proves that the construction cannot be the same as that formed by *ne* with the perfect. But the classes of verbs found in this construction form as strong an argument in favor of my interpretation as they form against the common interpretation. It will be noticed that of the 10 verbs in this construction in Cicero, 8 are verbs of mental action or of saying. By referring to the sections on the potential subjunctive and the subjunctive of modest assertion in any of our Latin grammars, it will be found that in a similarly large majority of the examples there given the verbs belong to one or the other of these two classes. Roby calls attention to the striking predominance of such verbs in the potential mood (the term 'potential' being employed to include such uses as *nemo putet* 'no one would think'), and especially when the perfect tense is used, in his Latin Grammar, §1536 (cf. also Kühner, II, §46, p. 133). In §§1536–46 he gives a large number of instances of the perfect subjunctive in the 1st person and an equally large number in the 3d person, accompanied in both persons by negatives, and all explained as instances of the so-called potential (to be translated by 'would' or, in the 1st person, by 'should'). But instances of the 2d person, accompanied by a negative, exactly similar in everything other than in the person and showing the same striking predominance of verbs of the same sort, Roby, like all the rest, classifies with the perfect subjunctive, under the sections on prohibitions (v. §1602). The only exception I find is *nec laudaveris* (Cic. Leg. 3, 1), out of which, fortunately, no one could possibly make a prohibition. Why such a dearth of these perfects in the 2d person, when they are so very common in the

1st and 3d persons? The truth seems to be that they are plentiful enough, if we will only recognize them when we see them.

I hope it will be admitted that I have made good my claim that *neque* (*nec*) is never found in Ciceronian prose with a volitive subjunctive. If any one still clings to the belief that some of the clauses I have just been considering are volitive, then I would remind him again of the fact, an all-important one in this connection that, among all the clauses introduced by *ne* or *neve* and continued by the addition of a second verb (and there are, literally, hundreds of such clauses), *neque* (*nec*) is, with but a single exception in a second-rate writer, unknown to prose as a connective, and extremely rare in poetry, before the time of Livy. There are so many such clauses that this omission cannot be accounted for as a matter of chance. Until some one can explain the absence of *neque* (*nec*) from all the various clauses, dependent and independent, which alone are known to be volitive in feeling, we certainly have a right to insist that he shall exhaust all other possible explanations before ever recognizing *neque* as used with a volitive subjunctive in Ciceronian prose.

A word should now be said regarding the use of *nihil* (*nil*), *numquam*, *ne—quidem*, and *nullus* with the perfect subjunctive. They occur as follows:

NIHIL (NIL): Plaut. Mil. 1007 Hercle hanc quidem *nil* tu *amassis;* mihi desponsast; Rud. 1135 tu mihi *nihilum ostenderis;* Curc. 384 *Nil* tu me saturum *monueris.* Memini et scio; Ps. 232 *Nil curassis:* liquido's animo: ego pro me et pro te curabo; Most. 511 *Nil* me *curassis:* ego mihi providero; Cic. in Verr. 2, 1, 54, 141 *nihil* ab isto vafrum, *nihil* veratorium *exspectaveritis;* pro Mur. 31, 65 "*Nihil ignoveris.*" Immo aliquid, non omnia. "*Nihil* omnino gratiae *concesseris.*" Immo insistito, cum officium et fides postulabit; ad Att. 2, 9 *nihil* me *existimaris* neque usu neque a Theophrasto didicisse; ib. 4, 17 (18), 4 De me *nihil timueris*, sed tamen promitto nihil; ib. 5, 11 Tu velim Piliam meis verbis consolere; indicabo enim tibi; tu illi *nihil dixeris;* accepi fasciculum, in quo erat epistola Piliae; ib. 5, 21 A Quinto fratre his mensibus *nihil exspectaris;* nam Taurus propter nivis ante mensem Iunium transiri non potest; ib. 7, 8, 2 animadverteram posse pro re nata te non incommode ad me in Albanum venire III. Nonas Ianuar.; sed, amabo te, *nihil* incommodo valetudinis *feceris:* quid enim est tantum in uno aut altero die? ib. 8,

2 Nihil arbitror fore, quod reprehendas. Si qua erunt, doce me, quo modo effugere possim. *"Nihil"* inquies "omnino *scripseris"*; ad Quintum 1, 1, 4, 14 sed si quis est, in quo iam offenderis, de quo aliquid senseris, huic *nihil credideris, nullam partem* existimationis tuae *commiseris;*

NUMQUAM: Plaut. Capt. 149 Ego alienus? Alienus ille? Ah, Hegio, *numquam* istuc *dixis* neque animum induxis tuom; Sall. Jug. 110, 4 arma viros pecuniam, postremo quicquid animo lubet, sume utere, et quoad vives, *numquam* tibi redditam gratiam *putaveris;*

NE ... QUIDEM, NULLUS: Cic. Tusc. Disp. 1, 41, 98 *Ne* vos *quidem*, iudices ii, qui me absolvistis, mortem *timueritis* (cf. Tusc. Disp. 2, 13, 32 Te vero ita adfectum *ne* virum *quidem* quisquam *dixerit*); Plaut. Bacch. 90 Ille quidem hanc abducet: *nullus* tu *adfueris*, si non lubet; Ter. Hec. 79 Si quaeret me, uti tum dicas: si non quaeret, *nullus dixeris.* It is customary to treat these as prohibitions, but it is practically certain that some of them are not volitive in character. It will be noticed that in most of these instances the verbs are such as indicate mere mental activity, which in itself practically decides the case against interpreting them as volitive subjunctives. Not only that, but whereas we found that *ne* with the perfect was in classical times used only in familiar, every-day address, and was carefully avoided on dignified occasions, in the passages under discussion there are repeated instances of the perfect subjunctive on such occasions. Take, for example, *nihil exspectaveritis* in Verr. II 1, 54, 144. If this were taken as a prohibition belonging to the same class as *ne* with the perfect, it would, as shown in Part I of this paper, be abrupt and harsh in tone, and not at all calculated to make a favorable impression upon the *iudices* to whom it is addressed. But under the other interpretation it would be very deferential and complimentary in tone. The expression 'you would (of course) expect nothing' implies full confidence in the good sense and judgment of the *iudices*, and would in every way be appropriate to the occasion. The passage from Cic. Tusc. Disp. is shown, by the Greek passage of which it is a literal translation, to be equivalent to χρή with the infinitive. In the only instance, then, where positive proof of this nature is at hand, my objection to regarding similar constructions as belonging to the volitive subjunctive is shown to be well founded. There is, to be sure, no serious objection to interpreting some of these as *bona fide* prohibitions. It is possible even that some of them are in the future perfect indicative. There does not seem to be evidence enough at hand to settle absolutely each individual case.

APPENDIX.

I ought perhaps to say a word regarding the use of prohibitive expressions in Silver Latin. It will be noticed that I have several times referred to Livy as marking the time when new constructions began to appear. Any one who has taken pains to examine any work on Latin Style, treated historically (e. g. that of Schmalz in Müller's Handbuch), must have noticed that Livy is very distinctly an innovator. New constructions, new words, new phrases, new ways of putting things fairly swarm into literary prose through the pages of Livy. He may be said in some respects to mark the beginning of the period of decline. This must be my excuse for classing him here with the writers of Silver Latin. So far, however, as the usages I have been considering are concerned, he seems to depart from what we have found to be the standards of classical prose only in one important particular, viz. he occasionally uses *neque* (*nec*) instead of the classical *neve* (*neu*) in clauses introduced by *ne*. This use of *neque* (*nec*) occurs as follows: 2, 32, 10 . . . conspirasse inde *ne* manus ad os cibum *ferrent, nec* os acciperet datum, *nec* dentes, quae conficerent; 3, 21, 6 dum ego *ne* imiter tribunos *nec* me contra senatus consultum consulem renuntiari *patiar;* 4, 4, 11 Cur non sancitis, *ne* vicinus patricio sit plebeius *nec* eodem itinere *eat, ne* idem convivium ineat, ne in foro eodem consistat? 26, 42, 2 . . . periculum esse ratus, *ne* eo facto in unum omnes *contraheret, nec* par esset unus tot exercitibus.

This use of *neque* (*nec*) in Livy in volitive clauses will perhaps cause greater uncertainty than would be felt in Ciceronian times regarding the correct explanation of certain other uses of *neque* (*nec*) with the subjunctive. It is, however, difficult, when one compares the instances of *neque* (*nec*) with the perfect subjunctive presented by Livy with the similar cases in Cicero, to resist the conclusion that they are to be interpreted in the same way. For the convenience of those who wish to make a comparison with earlier usage, I append a list of the prohibitive expressions found in Livy, including these questionable instances of *neque* (*nec*).

Ne with Perfect Subjunctive.

7, 34, 5 *ne dederis* (addressed by a tribune to a consul at a time of great emergency); 7, 40, 12 *ne destiteris* (addressed in bitter irony by the consul to the leader of mutinous soldiers); 9, 34, 15 *ne degeneraveris* (uttered by a tribune in a tirade against Appius Claudius for refusing to give up office at the expiration of his term); 10, 8, 6 *ne fastidieris* (earnest plea for his rights which had been denied); 21, 44, 6 *ne transieris* (Hannibal working on the passions of his soldiers, by quoting the arrogant demands of the enemy); 22, 49, 8 *ne* funestiam hanc pugnam morte consulis *feceris* (appeal for the life of the consul); 30, 30, 19 *ne* tot annorum felicitatem in unius horae *dederis* discrimen (Hannibal to opposing general, Scipio); 31, 7 *ne aequaveritis* (not a prohibition, but a concession) Hannibali Philippum, ne Carthaginiensibus Macedonas. Pyrrho certe aequabitis. Aequabitis dico? Quantum vel vir viro vel gens genti praestat! 40, 14 *ne miscueris* (Demetrius, who had been accused of trying to murder his brother, in tears, addressing his father, who is acting as judge).

Neque (nec) with Perfect Subjunctive.

5, 53, 3 *nec* id *mirati sitis* (addressed to the Quirites); 21, 43, 11 *nec existimaveris* (Hannibal to his soldiers); 23, 3, 3 *nec* quicquam raptim aut forte temere *egeritis;* 29, 18, 9 *neque* in Italia *neque* in Africa quicquam gesseritis (addressed to the *patres conscripti*).

Numquam, nusquam with Perfect Subjunctive.

Livy 1, 32, 7 *numquam siris* (addressed to Jupiter); 21, 44, 6 *nusquam* te *moveris.*

Ne with Present Subjunctive.

44, 22 rumores credulitate vestra *ne alatis* (Weissenborn).

Neque (nec) with the Present Subjunctive.

22, 39, 21 armatus intentusque sis *neque* occasioni tuae *desis neque* occasionem hosti *des.*

Neque with Imperative.

22, 10, 5 *neque* scelus *esto* (probably = 'and it shall be no crime,' the negative spending its force upon *scelus*).

Ne with Imperative.

3, 2, 9 *ne timete.*

Noli with Infinitive.

7, 24, 6 *nolite expectare;* 7, 40, 16 *nolite* adversus vos *velle* experiri; 10, 8, 5 *noli erubescere;* 32, 21 *nolite fastidire* (twice); 34, 4 *nolite existimare;* 34, 31 *nolite exigere;* 38, 17 *nolite existimare;* 38, 46 *nolite existimare.*

Cave with Present Subjunctive.

5, 16, 9 *cave sinas;* 8, 32, 8 *cave mittas;* 22, 49, 9 *cave absumas;* 30, 14, 11 *cave deformes* et *corrumpas.*

My statistics for Silver Latin proper cover only Phaedrus, the tragedies of Seneca, Tacitus and the Declamationes that commonly go under the name of Quintilian. They have, however, been so hurriedly gathered that I will not vouch for their completeness, though the omissions cannot be many. My examination of these authors leads me to think it probable that the principles I have laid down for classical times will, in the main, hold also for Silver Latin, though, as we should expect, in view of the general breaking up of classical standards, exceptions are more common. Prohibitions (including, as usual, the instances of *neque* [*nec*]) occur, in the works mentioned, as follows:

Ne with the Perfect Subjunctive.

Phaedrus: App. 11 *ne* istud dixeris (gymnast to a man who had questioned his strength); 26, 5 *ne timueris* (countryman to a hare).
Seneca: none.
Tacitus: Ann. 6, 8 *ne* patres conscripti *cogitaveris;* Hist. 1, 16 *ne* territus *fueris* (Galba to his successor in office, familiarly grasping his hand); 2, 77 *ne* Mucianum *spreveris* (Mucianus to Vespasian).
Quintiliani (?) Declam.: none.

Neque (nec) with Perfect Subjunctive.

Phaedrus: none.
Seneca: none.
Tac. Hist. 2, 47 *nec* tempus *computaveritis;* 2, 76 *nec expaveris.*
Quintiliani (?) Declamationes 249 *neque negaveris* (three times); 257 *neque spectaveris.*

Nihil with Perfect Subjunctive.

Tacitus: Ann. 16, 22 *nihil* ipse *scripseris*.

Ne with Present Subjunctive.

Phaedrus and Seneca: none.
Tacitus: Dial. 17 *ne dividatis*.
Quintiliani (?) Declamationes 306 *ne* quid improbe *petas*.

Neque (nec) with Present Subjunctive.

Phaedrus, Seneca, Quint. (?) Declam.: none.
Tac. Ann. 3, 50, 5 *nec metuas;* id. ib. 6, 8 *nec adsequare*.

Ne with Imperative.

Seneca: Thyest. 917 *ne parce;* 984 *ne metue;* Phoen. Frgm.
495 *ne verere;* 556 *ne erue neve everte;* 645 *ne metue;* Phaed.
136 extingue *neve praebe;* 227 *ne crede;* 1002 *ne metue;* 1249
ne metue; Medea 1024 *ne propera.*

Noli with Infinitive.

Phaedrus: 1, 25 *noli vereri;* 2, 3 *noli facere;* 3, 18 *noli adfec-
tare;* 4, 7 *noli esse.*
Quintiliani (?) Declamationes 247 *noli mirari;* 315 *nolite dare;*
375 *noli dicere.*

As regards the use of *non* in Silver Latin, I believe that it still
continued to be carefully distinguished from *ne*. It will be found
that some of the supposed instances of *non* in the sense of *ne* may
be explained by understanding the *non* to spend its force upon
some particular word[1]; and that the others, without exception,
become perfectly clear if the subjunctive concerned is understood
as one denoting obligation, or propriety, of which *non* and *neque*
are the regular negatives. To this latter class belong, for instance,
Sen. Q. N. 1, 3, 3 *non dubitaveris;* Rutil. Lup. II 9 *non credideris;*
Sen. Ep. 99, 14 *non imperemus;* Quint. 1, 1, 5 *Non assuescat* ergo
sermoni, qui dediscendus sit; id. 7, 1, 56 *non desperemus;* etc.
Even the much-cited passage in Ovid: aut *non tentaris* aut perfice,

---

[1] This hypothesis will also explain the supposed occurrence of *non* with the
imperative in Ovid. No other author, I believe, has been suspected of such
barbarism; cf. Schmalz, Lat. Synt. 37; Kühner, Ausführl. Gram. d. Lat. Spr.
II, §48, 1.

may be explained in the same way: 'you should either not try at all, or else, if you do, effect your object.' An unjustified use has been made in this connection of Quint. 1, 5, 50 qui tamen dicat pro illo *ne feceris non feceris*, in idem incidat vitium, quia alterum negandi est alterum vetandi. This passage has been cited to show that *non feceris* is not good Latin, whereas it distinctly says that it is good Latin. Quintilian is merely trying to explain the difference in use between *ne* and *non*, as any one might do in a similar treatise. He does not even imply that *non* ever was used in literature in the sense of *ne*. All he says is that *if a man should so use it (dicat), he would make the same mistake*, etc. It is then probable that *aut non tentaris aut perfice* does not represent an error of a class to which Quintilian has been supposed to refer, but that it is a perfectly legitimate usage. Still, inasmuch as *neque (nec)* is found with the imperative mood in poetry, and inasmuch as there are undoubted instances in the prose of Silver Latin of *neque (nec)* in clauses of negative purpose, it must be admitted that there may be some doubt about my interpretation of *non* in some of the clauses cited from this period. But it seems to me that, to say the least, the probabilities are on my side.

www.ingramcontent.com/pod-product-compliance
Lightning Source LLC
Chambersburg PA
CBHW022159020726
47496CB00008B/2782